Journey to Fulfillment

Pawleys Island Paradise, Book 3

Laurie Larsen

Laurie Larsen,
EPIC Award-winning author of *Preacher Man*

Random Moon Books
A Phase for Every Fancy

This is a work of fiction. Names, characters, places, and incidents are either the product of the author's imagination or are used fictitiously, and any resemblance to actual persons living or dead, business establishments, events, or locales, is entirely coincidental.

Journey to Fulfillment
COPYRIGHT © 2015 by Laurie Larsen

All rights reserved. No part of this book may be used or reproduced in any manner whatsoever without written permission of the author except in the case of brief quotations embodied in critical articles or reviews.

All Content by author Laurie Larsen
Cover Art by Steven Novak
Formatting by Polgarus Studio
Published by Random Moon Books
Published in the United States of America

A Letter from Laurie …

Hello everyone! Thank you for joining me on this journey and thanks for visiting Pawleys Island one more time!

For *Journey to Fulfillment*, I decided it was high time to offer a book featuring a romance between a married couple. Most romance novels END at the engagement or the wedding. What, married couples can't have an interesting love story?

Stella's kidnapping and rescue at the end of Book 2, *Tide to Atonement*, provided the perfect opportunity to explore the impact that a personal tragedy can have on a stable, happily married couple. A couple who had never really faced adversity before. A couple who were as opposite in their approach as could be. Having just celebrated my own 25th wedding anniversary last year, it was very interesting to me to write this married couple romance. I hope you enjoy it.

What's next? For those of you who were wondering, the Pawleys Island Paradise series will NOT end after three books. I love writing these books! I've started just a snippet of Book 4 — which I've included as an excerpt at the end of this book. This will be Jasmine's story (Leslie's daughter). Although I haven't written much, it will start with Jasmine's graduation from college, which is the first opportunity for Leslie and Tim, her ex-husband, to be in the same room since their divorce in Book 1. Chance for possible fireworks? Or will Leslie be so happy and relaxed with Hank at her side that she'll leave Tim regretful for mistakes past?

Since Jasmine has so much free time on her hands now that she's done with school, she'll delve into solving a family mystery that involves her. And of course, she'll fall in love along the way. I'm already itching to get started on it.

So much excitement has surrounded this series. Ever since I priced Book 1 *Roadtrip to Redemption* as a free download in August of 2014, the e-book shot up to the top 5 (peaking at #1!) in its category and has stayed there. At this point, over eighty thousand people have downloaded it. Book 2 *Tide to Atonement* was released in September and has ranked consistently in the top 5 of its category until one miraculous week in November, **it hit #1!!** This lovely event allows me to add *"#1 Amazon Best Seller"* to my list of credentials as an author!!

God is blessing and anointing this series and I thank Him for that. And I thank you for being here with me!

Laurie

Acknowledgements

Every book takes a village and this one is no different. I rely very heavily on other authors in my trusted circle to read my treasures and point out ways to make it better.

My thanks to author Stephanie Reid with her background in counseling, for reading the scenes featuring Stephanie Reynolds, LCSW and making sure she sounded professional. And, the character took on Stephanie's name as well.

My boundless thanks to the talented authors of Random Moon Books. Especially for this book, the three that read it pre-release and provided infinitely helpful advice:

Genevieve Jack
L.J. Bradach
Katy Lewis

Love you all!

Other Christian Fiction Books by Laurie

The Pawleys Island Paradise series:
   Book 1: Roadtrip to Redemption
   Book 2: Tide to Atonement
   Book 3: Journey to Fulfillment

Laurie's 2010 EPIC Award Winner for Best Spiritual Romance: *Preacher Man*

Coming soon! Laurie's 15th anniversary special edition re-release of her very first published novel, *Whispers of the Heart*.

Previously on Pawleys Island Paradise ....

Jeremy and Emma were about a mile and a half out from the Last Known Position – the cabin's front yard. Sweeping back and forth over the terrain had proved monotonous and tiring but entirely necessary. Stella could be injured, unconscious, asleep, or hiding due to fear. She may not do what you'd expect her to do. They couldn't rely on her finding them, they had to locate her.

Emma heaved a big sigh. She looked at her feet and then got distracted. She kneeled to the ground, down on her knees and reached for something. "Jeremy. Take a look at this." She lifted a pink, fuzzy circle. "It's a scrunchie!"

He gave her a confused look.

"A ponytail holder! Like little girls wear. It's pink, to match the hat. It's been sitting here in the woods and it's not that dirty. Maybe it just recently fell here."

She stood up and the excitement in her voice and her face made his adrenaline pump. "Stella!" he called. And so did Emma, "Stella! Are you here? It's Uncle Jeremy! Stella!"

They bounded about the area with newfound enthusiasm, calling loudly. Then Emma did a "shhhh!" shushing sound and Jeremy shut up. "I think I hear something. Stella?"

Jeremy strained his ears. Then, he and Emma gasped and quieted, staring at each other as they dared to hope. Together, they heard it, a tiny voice saying, "Uncle Jeremy."

They searched frantically. The woods and undergrowth were heavy and unchecked in this area. If she were lying down on the ground, she'd be completely covered. She could be hunched behind a log, under a bush, up in a tree.

"Stella! Sweetie! Lift your hand! Can you do that, lift your hand and wave for me. I'll come get you."

Jeremy and Emma stood with their backs to each other, each scanning half the perimeter of a circle. Then Jeremy caught a motion. He pointed, "There!"

They dashed over just as Stella was trying to sit. He pulled her up and into his arms, and with Emma wrapping her arms around both of them, they all embraced. Stella was crying, Emma was crying, and soon Jeremy let loose with tears of relief as well.

"Oh baby, what happened to you?" He held her so tight he had half a fear he was squeezing the breath out of her, but she needed to know she was safe, she was in his arms and he'd never let anything happen to her again.

"Grandpa Joe said he would take me for a ride. He said Mama was at the store and called and told him to bring me there. I couldn't open the door. It wouldn't open." Her story took too much of a toll on her self-control and she sobbed wildly. Both Jeremy and Emma did their best to comfort her, rubbing her head, her back, covering her cheeks with kisses and telling her how much they loved her.

"When he got out of the car, I kept trying to open the door, but it wouldn't open, so I climbed into the back seat and got it open. I was going to jump out, but Grandpa Joe started the car. So I had to roll out while the car was moving." She sobbed again. "I hurt myself." She lifted her left ankle and pointed at it. It was swollen and bruised.

He placed his lips against her forehead. "You are the bravest little girl I know. I'm so proud of you." They stood there, the three of them, all connected, praying silent prayers of thanks.

"Uncle Jeremy?" Stella's tiny voice whimpered.

"Yes?"

"I'm thirsty. And I want my mommy."

Jeremy and Emma smiled at each other. Jeremy pulled his cellphone out of his pocket and called his sister. She answered on the first ring. He didn't even say hello. "We've got her." His sister's shouts were so loud he pulled the phone away from his ear and held it out for Emma and Stella to hear. Bringing it close to his mouth again, he interrupted her, "Here she is," and handed the phone to Stella to chat with her mama as they started the long hike back.

CHILD AMBER ALERT

Pawleys Island, SC: Five-year-old Stella Mueller, daughter of Tom and Marianne Mueller was abducted from her home at approximately 2:00 PM today. Her abductor, Gary Slotky of Myrtle Beach, has been apprehended by police, however Stella is still missing. Law enforcement and local search and rescue volunteers have been dispatched, covering a four-mile radius of the last known position. Stella is a Caucasian female, last seen wearing blue jeans, a pink jacket and pink ball cap. Slotky has been taken into police custody and charged with kidnapping of a minor child.

Chapter One

The cell phone went dead, crushing her fragile connection with her five-year-old daughter.

"Stella? Stella?" Marianne Mueller gasped, knowing the frantic tone in her voice would accomplish exactly nothing. She inspected the face of the phone, and it verified that the line was, indeed, lost. Suppressing the urge to stomp her foot on the silly thing into the grassy ground, she lifted her head and scanned the heavy foliage all around her.

Tom grabbed her shaking hands, effectively stopping her from hurling the cursed device. "We're in the middle of nowhere, Marianne." Her husband was always the voice of reason. Of course, it was a miracle they'd gotten Jeremy's call in the first place. Cell towers were sketchy in these parts, in the best of times.

Tom pulled her close and guided her head into his chest, his warmth and scent drawing her home. She gulped cleansing air, trying to hold off the tears threatening to make a fresh appearance. She'd cried all day. Well, of course she had. Her daughter was missing.

Kidnapped by a crazy man who was driving drunk in the car he hadn't even belted her into when he enticed her to take a ride with him.

"It's over now," Tom said. "We'll see her soon."

She concentrated on drawing in air, slowly. Yes. How would she have ever gotten through these endless hours of searching without his strength and level-headedness? A smile emerged through her tears. "Yes. She'll be in my arms and I'll never let her out of my sight again."

Tom pressed his lips against her forehead and pulled her tighter. "She's safe now. How'd she sound?"

She glanced at the phone again, and thought of the short phone conversation she'd shared with Stella. Somewhere on Pawleys Island, Marianne's brother Jeremy had found her baby. Safe and sound, although tired, hungry, dirty and scared. Hiding in the woods, trying to stay safe after escaping the crazy man.

She could only imagine the joyous celebration in the woods moments ago between Stella, Jeremy, and his girlfriend Emma. Jeremy's words over the phone, sharing the jubilant news, "We've got her." When Stella got on, they'd talked just long enough for Marianne to confirm that indeed, it was Stella. To ask her if she was okay, and to let her know that Daddy and Mommy loved her, oh so very much.

Stella had started a story about a little pink elastic scrunchie that had been in her hair, but had come loose when she'd pulled her Pawleys Island Pelicans baseball cap off and left it in the crazy man's car.

A sign? An assist to the dozens of volunteer searchers, friends and family members who were combing every inch of this island for some sign of precious little Stella? Her story continued, so Marianne didn't have time to ask.

The scrunchie held on through the adversity of hiking several miles alone through the woods, while Stella put distance between herself and the dangerous man. But it eventually fell loose and landed on the forest floor. And that

— that one random hair accessory was what led Emma, then Jeremy to find her.

Thank the Lord. Thank God for small miracles like pink scrunchies.

"She sounded wonderful. I mean, she's exhausted, she's starving, she's scared. But she's so happy to be safe, her ordeal over. You know her Uncle Jeremy is her hero, now more than ever."

Tom didn't respond but he kept up his strong hold on her shoulders. "Want to try calling her back?"

It was worth a try. She pulled back from him, tried a redial and waited with the phone on speaker. Silence, then one ring tone, then straight to some recorded message from the phone company. She sighed and disconnected.

"It's okay. I got to hear her. We'll just have to wait. Even if it kills us."

His lips gave a little grimace that she was sure was intended as a smile. "I assume he'll take her back to the Inn."

She nodded. They turned to make the trek to their car and ran into one of the rescuers in charge. "My brother found her. She's safe. He's bringing her home. Thank you for everything."

A grin lit the man's face. She was sure he had some mountain of announcements, process and paperwork to follow now that the search was over. But he could initiate that. She had a daughter to wait for.

* * *

At least forty minutes had passed from the time they got the call, till they now sat waiting at the Seaside Inn, their home and place of business. Sharing their home with up to a dozen vacationing families was both a blessing and an inconvenience, depending on the situation. Tonight, word had spread among the vacationers, mostly retired snowbirds. Six or eight of them waited anxiously in the great room. Stella was a favorite among all guests, with her easy socialness, her happy smiles and her expert sand castles out back on the beach.

"They found her," Tom announced immediately, and a rush of relief filled the room, murmurs of thanks to God for many answered prayers. "She's on her way now."

After hugs and pats on the back by loving well-wishers, the room cleared, leaving Tom and Marianne. She checked her watch. "Do I have time for a shower, you think?"

"Sure. Make it quick."

She nodded and headed to their family's wing of the inn, separate from the guest rooms. She dug in her purse for her key, then pushed through the door, pulling clothes off on the way to the bathroom. She couldn't bear it if Stella arrived while she wasn't there to greet her. Her baby — her only child. A shudder wracked her shoulders. She couldn't protect Stella from the evils of the world — *obviously* — but she sure could show her with words and actions how much she loved her.

She stepped into the hot spray and lifted her face. Jets pinged off her forehead and eyelids as she started a silent prayer. *Thank You, God. Thank You for bringing Stella safely home. She's my life. My child that You have entrusted to me.*

She turned, her back now to the firm fingers of water. *I didn't do a good job of keeping her safe. I failed her, and You. The evils of the world grabbed her from me. I was no match but I will be. I will be, God. Stella is my top priority, and I will keep her safe, no matter what. With Your help. I'm sorry. I'm sorry, God. Help me do better.*

The tears hit with a vengeance then, and she couldn't keep up with the silent prayer. Sobs wracked her middle and her legs gave out, no longer able to hold her. She bent her knees and slid down the wall of the shower till she hunched in the corner, weeping.

* * *

Despite her watery meltdown, she made it out to the great room before Stella arrived. Tom sat in an easy chair in the corner, his leg crossed over one knee, his fingers picking at a stray string on his shoe. He looked up. "I called Jeremy about ten minutes ago. We're both back in range, so I reached him."

"And?" Her heart was in her throat, she couldn't help it.

He smiled slightly. "She fell asleep in the back seat."

"Ahhh. She's exhausted." Of course she was. She spent at least five hours tromping through the cold woods after her escape from her prison. No food. "I wonder if Jeremy stopped to get her something to eat."

Tom shook his head distantly. "He didn't mention it."

Marianne stood up and took a step toward the kitchen. Tom looked up at her, alarmed. "They're only moments out."

Priorities warred within her. She could make Stella's favorite peanut butter and apple sandwich in less than two minutes. But the price was too high if it meant not being here to greet her little girl.

The door flung open. Jeremy, carrying Stella in his arms, flanked by Emma, strode into the room. Marianne squealed.

"Mommy," Stella said, eyes closed and arms out. Marianne pulled her into an embrace, giving her brother a grateful expression. He knew. No words were necessary.

Tom joined them and wrapped his arms around his family. He murmured words into Stella's bent head, her unrestrained hair creating a curtain around her face. The two of them had such a bond. Before long, her daughter was laughing.

Stella threw her head back and for the first time, Marianne saw a glimpse of her happy, undamaged little girl. She planted a kiss on Stella's cheek and Stella struggled to get down on her own feet. No more pampering for this little fireball. Marianne squeezed her one more time to savor the closeness, and slid her down to the floor.

Jeremy stood with his hand on Emma's shoulder. "Well, we'll get going and let you guys do your thing."

"Yeah, good idea," Tom said abruptly. Marianne looked over at him, surprised by his brusqueness. If it weren't for Jeremy, Stella could still be lost. Then again, Tom had searched endlessly and was undoubtedly tired. Too tired for politeness. And she looked forward to having Stella to themselves. So, Marianne moved to Jeremy and wrapped her arms around both him and Emma. "I can't thank you enough."

Jeremy shook his head. "No need. Glad it worked out the way it did."

She pulled away. "Of course it did. I wouldn't have survived if it didn't."

Emma reached for her hand and squeezed it, her face a mess of emotion. "I'm so sorry, Marianne. I can't even imagine what he was thinking."

Marianne lifted her hand. "Sweetie, I can't talk about it now. I can't even think about it now. Please. I don't hold anything against you, but … he needs help, you know."

Emma gave her head a firm shake. "Yes, he does. The police took him to jail, which is where I imagine he'll stay for a while."

Marianne pulled the girl into her arms. "That's good enough for now."

"Oh yeah," Jeremy said. "Normally we'd all have to go to the police station to give our statements, but they were willing to let that wait till tomorrow, since Stella's so young, and so tired."

Marianne looked over to Tom. "We have to take her to the police station tomorrow?" He rolled his eyes and she swung her gaze back to her brother.

"Yes," Jeremy replied, "but hopefully for just a short interview. She'll do better after a good night's sleep."

A shudder flitted down Marianne's spine. A kidnapping. Search and rescue. An Amber Alert. Marianne was in way over her head, but she had to be strong for Stella. She planted a happy smile on her face and chanted, "Say goodbye to Uncle Jeremy, Stella, and a thank you very much!" She ignored the odd look from Tom.

Stella obliged, and soon the room was quiet with the three of them. Tom sat back on the easy chair and pulled Stella on to his lap. Marianne kneeled in front. Her daughter was filthy. But she couldn't count the number of hours she'd gone without a meal, so she'd leave it up to her.

"Sweetie, do you want something to eat first, or do you want a bath?"

Stella's eyebrows shot up as she considered her options, raising an index finger to pat on her lips. "Hmmm," she said, as if she were at a toy store surveying the inventory, "ice cream?"

Marianne chuckled. "Food first, it is. But not ice cream, not on an empty stomach. You'll end up with a tummy ache all night. How about a nice sandwich first, then ice cream, *then* a bath?"

Stella smiled, and nodded. Marianne stood, intending to head for the kitchen, but Tom caught her hand. Marianne looked back, and then took Stella's hand with her other. He said, in that soft voice of his so full of heart, "Sweetheart, we love you so much and we're so glad to have you back, safe and sound."

Marianne added, "We're so sorry you went through that, baby. We'll never let something bad happen to you again."

Tom gazed at her, the expression on his face surely supposed to be a message. But she hadn't the strength to figure out what it was, and she was more concerned with Stella's feelings at the moment.

"Stay right here, baby. I'll be back in a flash."

Chapter Two

The night was short and fitful with one extra person in their bed, albeit a small person. Stella was always working the angles and one of her favorite requests was to sleep in Mommy and Daddy's bed. The answer was usually a firm no. But she and Tom were both willing to make an exception for this night.

The late night nap in the car, plus the big meal, topped off by a double dose of sugary ice cream, all contributed to Stella's restlessness. Add in a lack of space on their mattress, and the tossing and turning of all people involved, and Marianne was certain that no one slept well. She pulled the covers back, ready to give up the fight with slumber. She could use a little quiet time to pray and think, and an infusion of coffee to get her day started.

She glanced at the clock on her bedside table: 4:10. Earlier than she usually arose, but not outrageously so. Pulling a robe off the chair beside the bed, she slipped it on and tiptoed toward the doorway. Turning, she looked back at the two people who made up her world. Both slept soundly at the moment, so she closed the door behind her.

At the door to their suite that led out to the public part of the Inn, she hesitated. Normally, they never locked it while they were in the Inn. But then again, they'd never before had their daughter kidnapped from beneath their noses. Maybe they needed to institute some stricter security measures. She went and found her purse, grabbed her suite key from it and slipped it in her pocket. Leaving the apartment, she made sure the lock was set and pulled it firmly.

She walked to the back porch where she offered coffee and pastries for their guests every morning. Some mornings, she'd bake; others, her chef would prepare the pastries. Rarely, she'd run out to the bakery and buy pre-made goodies. Today would definitely be a bakery day.

She put on the coffee and had a seat on the wooden screened-in porch, facing the ocean. Darkness still covered the water so she couldn't quite see it, but she could hear it. And smell it. And feel it. She was a beach girl, born and raised. Years and years of running out the back door and across the hot sand, bare feet burning till she reached the water's edge and dunked them in cool salt water. Just like she was raising her daughter. There wasn't a better way to grow up, or at least, she hadn't experienced it. Her mind wandered to friends who'd grown up in a city, in a suburb, on a farm, in the mountains. None of it compared to her childhood on the Atlantic Ocean and the white sand beaches.

She sat quietly, sipped her coffee, listened to the waves and eventually, watched the sunrise. Memorized snippets of prayer ran inside her head. She murmured her own heartfelt words. Her thankfulness for Stella's safe and healthy return was overwhelming, but she couldn't help but wonder why, oh why did her little girl have to go through that terrifying experience to begin with? And what long-term effect would it have on her? What new terrors were planted into her previously carefree daughter that weren't there before? How could Marianne help her? How could she avoid disaster in the future?

About 6:30, a beach walker bundled in a hoodie sweatshirt strode along the side of the Inn and on to the vast expanse of sand behind it that led to the shoreline. Marianne watched the figure in the growing dawn. It was a slim person, probably a woman, head covered by a hood and carrying a stack of white boxes tied together by string.

Bakery boxes?

The figure made her way up the big boardwalk that led from the beach toward the Inn and finally ended up just outside the porch's door. She spotted Marianne inside and waved, pushing her hood back to reveal ... it was Leslie.

"Oh, my gosh!" Marianne jumped to her feet and opened the door, moving aside to let her in. "What are you doing here so early?"

Leslie stepped in and deposited her stack of boxes on the long wooden table inside the porch. She shucked off her sweatshirt, shaking out her arms. She leaned into Marianne and brushed a kiss across her hair. "Praise the Lord." Leslie's smile was deep and genuine.

And even though she wasn't Marianne's real mom, she was a step mom, which was just good enough. If her mom were alive, she would've done the same thing.

Leslie opened her arms, Marianne stepped into them and let the tears fall on Leslie's shoulder, while Leslie shushed and patted her and let her cry it out.

When the emotion had passed, they sat together in wooden Adirondack chairs facing the ocean waves and sand. Marianne used the terry sleeve of her robe to rub the moisture out of her eyes. "No more tears. I have to think of Stella now, and what she needs."

"Yes, you do. Eventually. But first, let's just celebrate the fact that your little girl is home. Without a scratch. Right?"

Marianne nodded. "Nothing that a good meal and a hot bath and a good night's sleep didn't fix. Physically." She let that last word hang out there. Because it wasn't necessarily the physical ailments that would be the hardest to repair.

"I'm so happy to hear it." Leslie patted Marianne's hand, then popped up and walked over to the table. When Marianne saw she was sliding the white string off the bakery boxes, she stood too, but Leslie waved her back. "No, you sit and relax. I'm going to set all these out for your guests, then get one and a delicious cup of coffee for myself."

Marianne settled back into her chair. "That's so sweet of you."

Leslie shook her head with a smile. "What's family for?"

Family. She and Leslie had officially become family last summer when her dad, Hank had surprised Leslie with a wedding. Not only had he planned the whole thing on his own, invited friends and family from near and far, but actually pulled it off, holding it in the old wooden beach house on stilts, The Old Gray Barn, that he and Leslie had co-bought and closed on that very day. Love makes a man do uncharacteristic things, and that was sure true for her father. He was always a wonderful husband to her mom, and an exceptional father to her, Jeremy and her sister Sadie, now living in Colorado. But his courtship and marriage with Leslie was an extraordinary thing. Marianne couldn't be happier for him finding his second happily ever after, and she was pleased to call Leslie family.

Leslie finished her preparations, then selected her muffin and poured a cup of coffee. Marianne refilled her cup and grabbed a donut.

"So, we heard it was Jeremy and Emma who actually found her last night."

"Yes, it was just starting to turn dark. They first found her pink scrunchie, then they realized it was a clue. They called and called her name and finally they connected. Stella had evidently laid down in the woods and wasn't visible unless you knew where you were looking."

Leslie shook her head in wonderment. "Isn't that something? It had been hours, right?"

"Yes. Five hours or so. My poor baby." Marianne stretched her legs out, trying to remove the achiness from the physical toll her searching had played on her body yesterday. "Did you hear it was Gary Slotky — Emma's father — who kidnapped her?"

Leslie's mouth dropped open, horrified. "What?"

"Snatched her right off the beach while she sat there happily digging sandcastles. He'd evidently befriended her, made her think he was nice."

Leslie shook her head. "Is she still sleeping?"

Marianne nodded. "With her daddy."

Leslie smiled. "She might want to milk that one for a while. Can't blame her."

Marianne looked away. "I'm having a real hard time with this. The pure evil of that man — Emma's father — right in our backyard. This feud between him and Jeremy had nothing to do with Stella, with us. But he involved her. He dragged her into danger, and I couldn't do a thing about it."

Leslie shook her head. "No, you couldn't. There's absolutely nothing you could have done. God puts us on this earth to live our lives, to follow Him and to help each other. We keep our eyes fixed on Him as best we can. But sometimes the real world intercepts. Pulls us into danger and evil that have nothing to do with us."

"But my little girl. She didn't deserve any of this."

"You're right. But God kept her safe. He placed Jeremy right where He did, so Jeremy could find her and bring her back to you. God was watching out for her. It could've been a lot worse, and I hesitate to even think about the damage that sick man could have caused."

Marianne stilled. Her brother Jeremy had been through the wringer over the last few months, with his release from prison, and falling in love with the daughter of a man who had been a victim of Jeremy's crimes a decade ago. Emma's father had been an employee of Harrison and Son, the company that Hank had operated most of his life, that Jeremy had worked to expand into bigger and pricier jobs when he'd graduated from college. Until he made some bad business decisions and ran the entire company into bankruptcy. He had to lay off all his staff, and new jobs were hard to come by. Emma's father maxed out his unemployment benefits, then settled into a life of laziness and alcoholism.

Jeremy beginning a relationship with his only daughter was the action that pushed Slotky over the edge of sanity and led him to sabotage her brother: acts of vandalism on his custom-made furniture business, setting fire to his inventory which was stored in the shed behind Marianne and Tom's Inn, and finally, kidnapping Stella.

"You know Leslie, as much as I consider myself a loving, peaceful person, I wouldn't hesitate to go all Mama Bear on his butt if he hurt my baby."

Leslie raised her eyebrows, then snorted. "I'd have to say, I'd put my money on Mama Bear in that fight."

"The Bible tells us to forgive. But I don't think I'll ever forgive him for what he did to my family. I hope he gets the book thrown at him and spends a good long time in jail."

Leslie put her hand on Marianne's. "It's too fresh. Take some time. Maybe you can pray later for God's help in finding forgiveness for him."

They settled into a comfortable silence and finished their morning snacks. Leslie looked over at her. "Do you mind me asking a question? Are you upset with Emma at all about her dad?"

"No!"

Leslie studied her face, and didn't respond.

"No, not at all. This has nothing to do with Emma. You can't control the actions of a family member. And I want Jeremy to be happy. He deserves that."

Leslie nodded. "Okay. Good." She smiled, then stood. "Well, your dad and I want to make ourselves helpful around here so that you and Tom can spend some time with Stella and take care of her needs. I've put in for a few days of personal time at school, and your dad postponed a couple of jobs he had on the books. So we are at your service."

Marianne put her hand on her heart. "Oh Leslie, that's so generous of you. I can't let you do that."

"Of course you can. You rely on your family in your time of need. Now, it's still early. Why don't you go on back to bed, catch another hour or two of sleep, and come back when you're feeling rested. I'll take care of everything till then, and Hank's coming over around eight. You and Tom can give us a training session a little later."

As much as her conscience was nudging her to turn down the help, her heart knew she needed and wanted time in the bosom of her little family. "I can't thank you enough."

"No need. Go on, now. I've got work to do!"

Marianne headed back to the suite, unlocked the door, locked it again behind her, and headed back to bed.

* * *

She ran through the woods. Leaves whipped her face, vines encircled her ankles, threatening to pull her down to her knees. Down into the thick forest floor covering where she'd disappear, never to be found again. The ground opened and tried to swallow her but she kicked and screamed and clawed. She wouldn't allow it; she had to find her baby, she had to fight against the evil forest before it swallowed her whole.

"Stella! Stella! I'm here, Mommy's here!"

A whimper floated to her on a breeze and she stilled. Quiet, quiet to hear the noise. Was it Stella?

But in her stillness, the forest apprehended her, pulling her, grabbing her, binding her. Is this what had happened to her precious Stella? Could she save her? Could she protect her? Or had she failed at the job?

"Stella!"

Strong arms pulled her body, but not down — up. Away from the forest floor, away from the fear. She opened her eyes and looked into Tom's. "Marianne, it was a nightmare. You're okay."

She shook her head and glanced around the room. She was in her bedroom, morning light had dawned and she was tousled in the covers. Tom held her. "What?"

Suddenly she heard sobs close by. Stella sat in the chair beside the bed, crying. "Oh baby, why are you crying? Come here, baby."

Tom loosened his grip. "You scared her to death, Marianne. You were screaming her name and you startled her."

Dismay crashed over her. The last thing she'd want to do is scare her daughter more, when it was now her job to

comfort her, to help her recover from the fear. She held her arms out and was gratified to see Stella crawl onto the bed and into her embrace. She did the best she could, shushing and stroking her hair and brushing the tears from her face while Tom sat nearby, watching. She made eye contact with him over Stella's head and his brow furrowed. He watched her guardedly, probably wondering if he had two special needs on his hands now, or if they would partner to help their daughter together.

"I'm sorry, Tom," she murmured. "It was just a nightmare."

He nodded. "Pretty violent one. Night terrors, maybe. You were sitting up, pushed up against the wall, screaming. It was frightening."

She shuddered and took a deep breath. "No wonder I terrified her. I'm so sorry."

He shook his head and reached out, rubbed her arm up and down. "Not your fault. But between the way you're handling it, and the way Stella is, I'm starting to wonder if we should go visit a counselor. What do you think? To at least get advice on how to best recover from this?"

She gazed at him with new eyes. This suggestion was totally unlike him. Tom had never been to counseling, or probably ever imagined a situation in life that he'd need to. He was more a man of action than thoughts, and touchy-feely emotions were definitely not in his wheelhouse. But obviously, his two girls were struggling, and through the night, she could imagine him turning over and over in his mind how best to help them, before coming up short and realizing that he didn't have the tools to do it himself.

"Yes. I agree."

He gave his head a single nod. That was decided, then. They had a plan of action, and now he could carry it out. She smiled, despite the solemnity of the mood. Her Tom. Methodical, logical, results-driven. She could always count on him. And she was thankful for it.

Stella pulled her head away from Marianne's chest. "Mom? Dad? I'm hungry."

Marianne smiled. "Great! That's good news. Because guess who is here and brought all kinds of great bakery goodies? Paw Paw Hank and Grandma Leslie!"

Stella squealed and scrambled off the bed.

"You get dressed, and I'll get freshened up and we'll all go out there together." Stella trotted away. She turned to Tom. "Dad and Leslie have taken a few days off work and plan to help out around the Inn so that we can spend dedicated time with Stella. We'll give them a little lesson on everything that needs to be done."

He didn't even hesitate. "Great. Very generous of them." And he readied himself for his day.

Chapter Three

They emerged from the apartment about fifteen minutes later, unable to convince Stella to wait any longer. A carefully coiffed ponytail was simply not as high a priority as greeting Paw Paw as soon as possible.

She ran loudly into the great room and launched herself into his arms. Fortunately, he was ready as he always was and he caught her, then spun her in a circle. Leslie watched from a short distance with a happy grin on her face.

"Aww, pumpkin, I'm so glad to see you safe and sound. The Good Lord answered our prayers last night, didn't He? He kept an eye over you and kept you safe from harm." Hank squeezed her close, and when he finally loosened his grip, he kept her right in his arms where he could keep an eye on her.

Within forty minutes, they had Stella set up at a table in the dining room with a chocolate chip muffin and a banana, and Tom and Marianne had schooled Hank and Leslie on the daily basics of managing the Inn. They covered how to make a reservation, how to check someone in, how to check someone out. How to settle a bill and how to take a credit card. How to answer the phone and respond to a variety of special requests. Who to call with housekeeping issues, who to call with dining room issues. How to seat the guests at dinner, and how to best help the wait staff with serving the meals. It was mainly common sense, but it did prompt Marianne to think that they should probably write this stuff down in an Innkeeping manual so that if she and Tom were ever absent, they could bring help up to speed quickly.

"Don't you worry about anything, you two," Leslie said. "We'll be fine. And your guests are so nice that if anything takes longer than usual, they'll understand."

"And we'll be here, too. It's not like we're leaving the premises," Tom replied.

"We'll grab you if we have questions. But your priority now is Stella."

Marianne gave a quick hug to Leslie, then to her dad. "We can't thank you enough."

Her dad patted her on the back. "Glad to help, darlin'."

Back in the living room of their private suite, Tom pulled out the phone book and flipped through it, using his index finger to scan the yellow pages. "Do you have a preference for our counselor?"

"No. I really don't know anyone in that field. Someone in Pawleys is preferable over having to drive to Myrtle."

"Yeah." He hunkered down with the book and she turned to Stella.

"Sweetie, Daddy's going to find us someone to talk to about what happened to you yesterday. Someone who can give us advice about how you're feeling and how to make you feel better."

She shrugged. "I feel okay."

"Sure, physically you feel okay. Your ankle isn't swollen anymore and you've rested and eaten. But how do you feel about what happened to you? Are you scared that it might happen again? Are you afraid to go back out on the beach and dig again? Are you afraid that someone else might try to grab you and put you in a car?"

"Marianne!" Tom's sharp tone came from across the room. She darted her head up in his direction.

"What?"

"You're scaring her."

She looked back at Stella, who did, now that he mentioned it, looked a little alarmed.

"Let's leave this to the professionals. They'll advise us how to deal with this."

A surge of irritation pulsed through her. "What, I'm not allowed to talk to my own daughter now? You think I'm going to damage her by speaking to her? You told me I scared her this morning when I was sleeping, and now you tell me I'm scaring her by talking to her?"

Even as the words came out of her mouth, she knew they were misguided at him. He didn't know any more about helping Stella than she did, but at least he was reaching out for help. But Stella was her daughter. If she couldn't talk to her normally like the mom she was, she would explode.

Tom was delayed from answering by a voice on the phone and his attention was drawn away. She turned to Stella and picked up her hands. "I'm sorry, sweetie. I definitely didn't mean to scare you. I just seem to be making mistakes today, so forgive me. You are safe and sound here in the Inn, and as long as you stay with me, Daddy, Paw Paw, Leslie or Jeremy, you will be protected. We will not let anyone get you again. Never. Okay?"

Stella nodded, her eyes wide and uncertain.

Tom hung up and walked over. "The counselor can get us in this afternoon. We'll go to the police station to give our statements now, then we'll probably have some free time till the appointment. How about we do something fun together — something Stella loves doing?"

Marianne turned her head to Stella and smiled big with excited eyes. "Mani/pedis!"

Stella squealed and clapped her hands. Tom said, "Huh?"

Marianne waggled her fingers at him, nails out. "A new polish for our toes and fingernails!"

He rolled his eyes good-naturedly. "You've got to be kidding."

"No Daddy! You'll love it! They can do your toes too!"

He grimaced and asked, "Do they have to paint them pink?"

Stella giggled with delight. "I don't think so, do they, Mommy?"

Marianne laughed. "No. Men usually just get clear."

"Then let's go!" Stella skipped to the door and flung it open. Marianne grabbed a jacket for her, and praised God that her little girl was so trouble-free. It was a good sign. On the way out, she grabbed Tom's hand and squeezed it. He gave a closed-mouth smile. She loved him. He was a good man and a good father, going to get pedicures on a perfectly good workday just to be with his daughter.

* * *

Forty eight hours ago, if anyone had told Tom he'd take a day off work in order to accompany his wife and daughter to the nail salon and then go talk about his feelings to a total stranger, he would've committed them to the asylum. Amazing the difference a day makes.

"It feels good, doesn't it?"

"Hmm?" He rolled his head in Marianne's direction, sitting beside him in her adjoining throne.

"So relaxing, huh?" She let her head fall back on the padded headrest and closed her eyes.

Tom looked down at the small woman working her little heart out, massaging his feet, oiling them, rubbing them, scrubbing them. He needed to tip her well. Whatever he was paying her wasn't enough. No one had ever gotten this up close and personal with his feet, his wife included.

"Yeah." Maybe he should get a pedicure more often. Then he snorted and glanced over at his resting wife. If he admitted that to her, she'd think he was the crazy one.

Stella was busy chattering with her pedicurist, and the young Asian woman was smiling and nodding. He gazed at his baby girl, the love of his life, and said a quick *thank you* to God for the tenth time today, for her safe return. She had had the scare of her life, but she'd returned to them safely. They'd given their statements to the police, who had put Slotky in custody. He'd do whatever he had to do to make sure she was well. This incident would not cause her lasting damage. He wouldn't allow it.

He let his eyes drift closed and his mind wander. It took a conscious effort to keep it from wandering back to the horror of the kidnapping and his fear of losing Stella. If anything had happened to his girl while she was in the grip of that maniac, God help him, he'd have to take matters into his own hands. God expected mankind to forgive their enemies, but that would be just a little too tall an order, in his opinion.

He sensed his blood pressure rising, his blood pulsing through his veins, at his choice of subject. He quietly breathed in, held the air and let it out. A few more, and he'd calm himself. No sense dwelling on tragedy. His Stella was back with them, in safe hands, and none worse for the wear. In an hour, they'd go talk to a counselor and figure out if she needed any help emotionally.

Thank You, God.

In an effort to keep his mind off the kidnapping, he forced it to concentrate on calm, ordinary subjects. Like his job, for instance.

His job as an Innkeeper was not a nine to five occupation. Obviously. The days started early and they ran late. And if a guest needed him in the middle of the night, he'd oblige.

When he and Marianne took the plunge eight years ago and bought the Seaside Inn, it was a dream and a hope. A dream come true for both of them to own a beautiful, rustic seaside hotel. A hope that they'd make it work without losing their shirts.

It was one of the things he loved most about Marianne — her willingness to try new things, and her unwavering determination to make it work. The early days were hard. Not only were they renovating the Inn, little by little (much of the work done by his father-in-law, Hank to save on costs), but they weren't filling all the rooms and maximizing their income. The Inn had been vacant for several years prior to their ownership so they had to get the word out.

Which they did … and with persistence and a little elbow grease, they developed a reputation for offering a fantastic beach vacation. The days of scraping month to month to make ends meet were over.

The Seaside Inn was their home as well as their livelihood. They rarely left it. Sure, they got burnt out sometimes with all the responsibility, but he wouldn't want his life any other way.

His pedicure ended sooner than his ladies'. They had to not only get color stroked onto their nails, then the evidently endless process of blowing them dry under some sort of fan contraption. He took advantage of the wait to call the Inn.

His father-in-law answered. "Hey Hank, it's Tom. How are things going?"

"Fine, just fine. Aren't you supposed to be enjoying some time off with your ladies?"

"Yes, you're right. But I have to admit, man-to-man, I'm going a little crazy here. We're been at the nail salon for over an hour and they're not even done yet."

Hank laughed. "This your first time to one of those fancy nail places?"

Tom pulled the phone away from his ear and gave it a dubious look before placing it back to his ear. "Well, of course it is. What do you think?"

Hank's chuckle continued. "Well, rest assured. Nothing has happened that Leslie and I haven't been able to handle. In fact, I've noticed some odd jobs that I could tackle for you during slow times, if you want."

Tom rolled his eyes. His father-in-law, the lifelong handyman. Not only could he do Tom's job with his hands tied behind his back, he had time leftover to make home improvements as well.

"Have at it, Hank. And thank you. I can't tell you how much we appreciate the help from you and Leslie." He was still laughing when he hung up.

"What's so funny?" Marianne and Stella were making their way over to the cashier, walking uncomfortably with their toes sticking up, pushed into odd, thin sandals. The price of beauty.

"Your dad. He must think we have it easy over there at the Inn. He's not only keeping up with the guests' demands, he thinks he has time to do some odd jobs he noticed."

She shook her head and shrugged. "Let him. He never sits, that one. He doesn't know the meaning of the word relax."

Tom paid the bill, tipped all three nail specialists and held the door for his family as they exited to the car. "Not bad," he admitted. "My feet have never felt or looked this good."

Marianne smiled at him. "I'll never tell."

* * *

Twenty minutes later, Tom pulled into the parking lot of the doctors' complex and found the office with "Stephanie Reynolds, Licensed Clinical Social Worker" etched into the glass door. After giving their name to the receptionist, Tom collected a clipboard containing about two hundred medical questions, and something called an informed consent form. He handed it directly to Marianne. She took it without question and began pounding out the answers.

The wait wasn't long before they were called back. Unlike what Tom was accustomed to — a sparse doctor appointment room with white walls, cold tile and an examining table — this office was a cross between a child's playroom and a sitting room in someone's home. No table, no desk, just comfortable chairs and a loveseat. And in the corner, a place for a child to sit on the floor and play with blocks or cars.

Stephanie Reynolds, LCSW sat on an easy chair with a folder in her lap, flipping through the mountain of forms

Marianne had just provided her. She looked up with a smile when they walked in.

"Welcome! So happy that you're here."

The woman sounded sincere and happy. He looked down at Stella. She loved adults in general, spending so much time with them at the Inn. She was comfortable and at ease around grownups. His heart warmed to see that her face turned into an easy grin at the counselor. He supposed it was part of Ms. Reynolds' job to build a rapport with children so they open up and talk.

Marianne and Tom sat on the sofa, and Stella climbed onto Marianne's lap. Stephanie hummed a faint tune under her breath as she finished studying the paperwork. Finally, she set the clipboard aside, looked up at them and presented a magnificent smile.

"So, here's how this will work. I'll talk with Stella for a while with you in the room. Please don't interrupt our conversation, but listen. At some point I may decide to excuse you and talk to Stella alone. At that point, you can walk back to the waiting room. We'll make further plans when I've had a chance to make a determination from my chat with Stella."

Marianne nodded, but Tom asked, "Will you ever interview my wife and I?"

"Possibly, but again, it'll depend on what I discover from Stella. All ready? Stella, please call me Stephanie."

Stella looked a little nervous, but hopefully the licensed professional could get her to open up and talk.

Stephanie held her hand out towards Stella. "Want to go sit on the floor and play with Legos?"

Stella grinned, nodded and jumped off her mom's lap. She settled onto the floor with crossed legs while Stephanie dumped a bucket of the plastic toys in front of her. Stella immediately dove into pushing one into the next, connecting them and soon forming a tall tower. Stephanie joined in, forming her own creation. Stephanie and Stella giggled as they competed on who could build the highest structure. Tom watched them play, and minutes ticked by. He was just starting to wonder how long play period would go on, when Stephanie started a conversation.

"I heard you had a scary experience yesterday, Stella."

His little girl nodded.

"Tell me what happened. First, how did you meet this man, what was his name?"

"Grandpa Joe. He helped me make my sand castles on the beach. He was really nice. At first."

"Where did he make sand castles with you?"

"On our beach, right behind the inn. I always go back there and dig and sometimes people help me. You know, people staying at the inn. I thought that's who he was."

"Do you go on the beach by yourself?" Stephanie asked.

"Yeah."

"But I always know where she is," Marianne said.

Stephanie's head came up in their direction. "It's okay. I'm not judging and I'd like to hear your recollection of the events in a few minutes, but for now, I'd like Stella to tell me what she remembers."

Tom put his hand on Marianne's knee and widened his eyes, his index finger over his lips in a "shhh" gesture. She whispered, "I don't want her to think Stella has free run over the whole place. She doesn't. I always know where she is, even when I'm busy inside."

Tom held his hand up in a stop motion. He turned back to the conversation.

"So how many times had this Grandpa Joe played sand castles with you?"

Stella sighed, looked up in the air. "Three. No, four. Four!" She shrugged. "Lots of times."

Tom's chest tightened as he thought about the man making periodic visits to his little girl, and Stella befriending him, just like she did every other guest at the inn. So trusting, so innocent. Why wouldn't she befriend him? He'd never want her to be suspicious of people.

And yet, now she had to learn to be. Innocence lost, at five years old. His hands tightened into fists as he struggled to control his temper.

"What did you and Grandpa Joe talk about? Did you talk much?"

Stella shrugged. "We talked sometimes. He said he had a little girl like me, only she's a grown up now. He said she was his favorite girl in the world, only now I'm one of his favorite girls too."

Tom shuddered. Grandpa Joe's girl — Emma — Jeremy's girlfriend. None of this would've happened — all of this would've been avoided — if Jeremy and Emma weren't dating. Had they not met, had they not gotten together, Emma's psychotic father wouldn't have concocted this elaborate scheme for destroying Jeremy. A scheme involving Stella, the little pawn in the middle.

"Grandpa Joe gave me a necklace."

"He did? When?"

"A little while ago. It had a pink sparkly stone."

Tom looked over at Marianne. She was staring at the conversation, looking nauseous. She shifted her gaze to him, and shook her head. He whispered to her, "The old man gave her a necklace? Did you ever see her wearing it?"

Marianne shrugged and shook her head.

The story continued, little by little. The man befriended her, gave her gifts, helped her build sandcastles, so that when it was time to entice her to get in the car with him, she followed him. Without a thought, without a doubt. Because he'd told her that Mommy had asked him to bring her somewhere, and Stella had believed him.

Thank God she was safe. Thank God he hadn't hurt her. But what price would she pay?

There were a few tears when Stella got into the scary part of the story — when she realized that Grandpa Joe was a bad man, and she was in danger. When his precious little five-year-old daughter realized that she had to fight for her life and try to escape. She was locked into the car, as it careened down the road, and she had to jump and roll to get out.

The tears weren't from Stella. Stephanie was doing a good job of keeping her calm and preoccupied with the Legos. No, the tears came from Marianne beside him.

He turned to her and her cheeks were wet, her lips trembling. He didn't want her to scare Stella again, so he stood, took her arm and guided her out the door into the corridor.

"I'm sorry," she said. She pushed her shoulders up and down, shook her hands out. "It was just so hard to hear all that, straight from her mouth. I can't imagine what she went through."

"We failed her, Marianne." Tom looked at her, eyes wide. "We didn't keep her safe. We let a stranger into our home and he befriended her, then kidnapped her. And we knew nothing about it. We failed her, you and I."

Marianne shook her head. "We won't let it happen again. We won't take our eyes off of her."

"But it happened once. Once too many."
"Are you saying it was our fault?"
"Ours. And your brother's."

Chapter Four

"Jeremy! This was Jeremy's fault? Have you lost your mind? Jeremy was the one who found her! We may not have her home safely if it wasn't for Jeremy."

"Lower your voice," Tom said, sounding tight and menacing. "You need to control yourself so we don't have another episode."

She shook her head, confused. "Episode?"

"Of you scaring Stella. Your tears and yells and over-the-top warnings are not helpful to her recovery. You need to remember that you're the adult here. For Stella's sake."

Marianne's first impulse was to argue, to blow up, to push back. Of course she was the adult here! What was he insinuating, that Stella was acting more like an adult than she was? But that reaction was exactly what he was warning her against. So instead, she scrubbed her hands over her closed eyes, took a deep breath and spoke with restraint and poise.

"What are you insinuating, Tom?"

He looked down at her and studied her face for some seconds before he answered. "You coddle your brother. It's unhealthy. And … you've scared Stella several times. That needs to end."

Marianne gasped. She wasn't used to accusations from her husband. They were a team — they were partners in every way possible. They raised Stella together, they ran their business together, they lived together, they loved each other. They were more often in sync than not, from a goals and vision perspective. They had similar views and they rarely argued.

Maybe he was so distraught over what had happened to Stella that he was taking it out on her. Understandable. Nothing so horrible had ever happened to them. However, she was crumbling apart. She needed him to be the strong one so she could lean on him. She had not quite considered that it would be the other way around.

"Tom, you're not thinking straight. Come on, now. Let's not attack each other. Let's lean on each other to get through this."

He looked like he was going to respond, thought better of it, and closed his mouth. Then, "We'll talk later. I want to hear the rest of Stella's answers."

He slipped back into the therapist's office. She watched the door close after him and she shivered. Her hands shook as she to wiped the new tears popping into her eyes. She was a hot mess. Her emotions were on the fritz over what had happened to Stella, and now Tom was being intentionally obtuse.

She'd try to give him a break. Maybe he was losing it as well. But it wasn't like Tom to place blame and make her feel bad. Once things settled down and life was more normal, she'd approach him about it. He'd most likely see reason and apologize. And things could get back to normal.

Meanwhile, she wiped her eyes, took a deep breath, shook out her arms, and went back into the office.

* * *

The appointment with the therapist took about ninety minutes, total. From Marianne's untrained eye, it appeared Stella was perfectly fine — her happy, well-adjusted little five-year-old daughter. However, she was interested in hearing what the professional thought.

Stephanie called in an assistant to play with Stella with the toys, and she sat in a far opposite corner of the room at a table, motioning for Tom and Marianne to join her. They took their seats, and she opened a notebook she'd used to take notes during her interview with their daughter.

"You'll be happy to know that I don't think Stella's going to have any long-lasting emotional impact from this incident."

Marianne let out a whoosh of relief, and reached across the table for Tom's hand. His unencumbered smile gave her hope that the real Tom was back. "So you're saying, no negative effects from the kidnapping?"

"I won't go so far as to say 'none,' but my assessment is that they are minor. And very treatable in a counseling environment."

Tom said, "Take us through the interview and tell us your assessment."

Stephanie nodded. "First of all, the fact that Stella was able to bond with me, an adult stranger she'd never met, and open up and answer my questions, is a good sign that she's not going to transfer her fear of one bad adult, to all new adults introduced into her life. That's a very encouraging sign. Next, I took Stella chronologically through the course of events. The fact that she could verbalize her original feelings of friendship for this man, that she liked him and thought he was nice, means that she can distinguish between good and bad. His bad actions didn't completely erase her fond memories she originally had for him."

"And that's a good thing?" Tom asked, sounding skeptical. "I'd rather have her hate the maniac for the rest of her life, than risk having her befriend him again."

"But Tom, he's been arrested," Marianne said. "She's not going to have to encounter him again."

"You don't know that. Our family has a connection to him. What if he's released? Found not guilty? Whatever. It's not like he's a random stranger."

There he went again with the accusation that Jeremy was somehow responsible for this crime. He wasn't. Not at all. Her brother had enough people discriminating against him because of his past. She'd be darned if she became one of them. Or allowed her husband to be one.

"I don't want to teach her to hate others. She's our sweet, loving girl. I'd rather not change that." She glanced over at Stephanie. "If at all possible."

Stephanie nodded. "Stella needs to distinguish between knowing the danger of this particular man, and of getting into dangerous situations like she did with this man, and avoiding those things. But if she can maintain her joy of life and enjoyment of adults and people in general, that will allow the healthiest recovery."

Marianne glanced over at Tom. He had clamped his mouth shut, but he wasn't through, she could tell.

"Go on, Stephanie, please," he said.

"My only other assessment is that Stella told the entire story of her abduction and being lost in the woods, and she never once broke down, cried or showed agitation."

"That's great," Marianne breathed with relief.

"Actually, this kind of emotional detachment may be the sign of a problem."

A problem? That she's happy? Marianne was sure her face reflected her confusion so Stephanie went on. "Feelings are okay. They are neither good nor bad, they just are. If Stella cries, that's understandable given what she went through. In fact, I'd like you both to be on the lookout for emotional outbursts. If you see her crying, please try the reflection technique. Say something back like, 'You were separated from us and you felt scared.' Reflection isn't about judging or trying to solve a problem. It's just understanding what emotion she's feeling, you see what I mean?"

Tom and Marianne both nodded.

"She did a good job of escaping and surviving, and she was found. She's back in the arms of her family, and she feels safe and loved. That's good. She may have nightmares or incidents of bad memories for a little while, but she's a very well-adjusted little girl, and I don't think she'll walk around in constant terror of being snatched again."

Marianne smiled. "That's wonderful."

"You two are good parents who have provided her with a loving home. That goes a long way toward fighting the fear resulting from an episode like this. Now, I would be remiss if I didn't order a short-term course of counseling sessions. I'll make them weekly, and the first three will be with Stella and me alone. In those future sessions, I'll be educating Stella about strangers, processing any lingering anxiety and giving her tools to feel empowered to squash those anxieties. Then, I'll plan a family session, with the four of us. After that, I'll re-evaluate and see if any more are needed. Your insurance should have no problem approving them."

They wrapped up, said good-bye and walked out to the car. At the back car door, before helping Stella up into her seat, Marianne kneeled and gave her a great big hug, holding her tight. "I love you, baby girl."

"I love you too, Mommy."

"We're so glad to have you back, safe and sound."

Stella nodded and climbed up into the car seat. "Can I go dig when I get home?"

'No,' was the first thing that popped into Marianne's mind, but instead she said, "Why don't we both dig together? We'll get our shorts and sunscreen on and go dig."

"Okay!"

* * *

Tom drove his wife and daughter home. Stella chattering in the backseat gave the illusion that all was well. He truly hoped her cheerful banter was a positive sign that the therapist's prognosis was accurate — that his dear Stella had escaped her trauma unscathed.

He glanced over at his wife. Her head rested on the seatback, her eyes closed. She let out a deep breath. He reached over and patted her hand. She jolted alert, then calmed as they met eyes.

"I think she'll be okay," he said softly.

Marianne darted a look into the backseat. "I hope so. But can you imagine if she isn't? Are we prepared to deal with whatever might come next if she isn't okay?"

He shrugged. "If we aren't now, we will be. What choice do we have?"

Marianne nodded. "She's our baby, and we'll do whatever is necessary to get her past this."

"But let's also be open to the possibility that she's just going to bounce back and everything will be back to normal."

"That would be such a miracle," Marianne murmured, then closed her eyes again, her lips moving quietly. Tom knew she was saying a silent prayer of thanksgiving. He let similar thoughts of gratitude pass through his mind.

Tom pulled into the sand parking lot in front of the Seaside Inn and they all piled out of the car. A big old pickup truck sat nearby, sturdy and work-worn. Jeremy's truck. A nauseous churn attacked Tom's stomach. He hadn't known his brother-in-law for long. He'd dated and married Marianne while Jeremy was away in prison. Last summer, he'd been released. He was a nice enough guy — very hard-working, remorseful over his mistakes of the past. Not looking for handouts, just wanted a fair shake to make his own way in the world.

Unfortunately, he seemed to attract trouble like a magnet attracts nails. Maybe all ex-cons experienced the same phenomenon — he hadn't honestly been around that many to know. But when Jeremy started dating Emma, layers of the onion started peeling away. Emma was the daughter of Gary Slotky, a man who had been laid off a decade ago, back when Jeremy was running Harrison and Son. Jeremy with his brand new Business degree, wanted to transform his dad's handyman business into something bigger and more profitable. Unfortunately, he was in over his head and resorted to making bad business decisions. When he ran the business into bankruptcy, he resorted to illegal measures to borrow money. He dug his hole deeper and never got out. Customers were cheated out of homes. Employees were laid off. Lives changed drastically as a result of Jeremy's activities.

Emma's father had held a grudge, had let his whole life fall apart because of his lay off — became an unemployed alcoholic, unwilling to get back on the ball and work again. For a decade, the name Jeremy Harrison was legendary in the Slotky family. The evil one, their scapegoat responsible for all the bad things in their lives. When fate put Jeremy and Emma together, Mr. Slotky couldn't deal with it. He schemed, keeping secrets from his wife and daughter, and started sabotaging Jeremy. Making him suffer, as Jeremy had made Gary suffer.

Sabotage of Jeremy's furniture inventory came first. Then arson of some of his wooden pieces being stored at the Inn. Finally, befriending Stella behind their backs and abducting her. It was over now. The man was arrested and taken to jail. And Stella was going to be fine. He had to believe that.

But the fact remained that, unintentional though it was, Jeremy stood at the root of all the danger and damage. God help him, if Stella had been injured or killed or traumatized, Tom would never be able to forgive Jeremy. Never.

But the question remained, could Tom forgive Jeremy now?

They walked in through the front door of the Inn. Leslie was standing behind the guest desk, studying the computer screen. Marianne went and gave her a kiss on the cheek. Stella reached her arms up and Leslie lifted her, settling her into a comfortable hold.

"So how was your day today, precious one?"

Stella held out her fingers, nails up. "Look! I got blue!"

"Just like the sky."

"And the ocean."

"You got it, sweetie." Leslie looked over the little girl's head at Marianne. "And how was the appointment?"

Marianne looked at Stella. "I don't know, what'd you think, Stella? How was the appointment with Stephanie?"

"It was fine. She was nice." Stella squirmed and Leslie let her down. "I'm going to go put on my beach clothes. You'll come out with me, Mommy?"

"I sure will. Come on back out here when you're done."

Stella scampered off back to the family suite. Marianne continued to Leslie, "The therapist said that Stella has suffered very little, if any, long-lasting damage or effects from the incident."

"Praise the Lord," Leslie exclaimed.

Tom stepped over to them. "Looks like we dodged a bullet on this one."

Leslie reached for his hands and squeezed them. "I'm so happy for you all."

Jeremy stepped into the great room from the sun porch. "Good news?" His face was hopeful. Marianne walked closer to him and put her hand behind his neck. "We think so. The therapist thinks she's going to be fine."

Jeremy pumped the sky with his fists and let out a celebration whoop. "Praise God."

"Yep," said Marianne and pulled him into a hug. Tom turned away.

Stella ran into the room wearing her shorts, flip flops and tee shirt. It was early March, and weather was unstable. Some days this time of year required long sleeves or jackets, and other days, the sun shone and bare arms and legs were fine.

And obviously his mind diversion tactics were working, if he was thinking about weather, as opposed to detesting his brother-in-law.

Stella noticed the hug going on in the great room and of course wanted a piece of it. She held her arms up, hopped up and down. Jeremy swept her up and landed her on his shoulders. Of course she laughed like it was the most fun she'd had in her life.

Marianne said, "Stella and I are going out to the beach to dig. Can you entertain her for a second while I go change my clothes?"

"Of course," said Jeremy.

After Marianne left, and Leslie answered the phone, it was the three of them. Jeremy bobbed at the knees, giving Stella a bumpy ride that caused a great deal of laughter. Jeremy looked over at him. "Great news from the therapist, huh?"

"Yep. She'll have a series of counseling appointments, but after the first one, things are looking good."

"Super. You and Marianne are fantastic parents. Stella knows she's loved."

Tom bit his bottom lip to refrain from saying something off the cuff he'd regret later. "She does, you're right. But she also feels safe here in her home, and that turned out to be untrue, didn't it?"

Marianne returned while Jeremy went motionless and blinked at him. "You ready to go, sweetpea?" Marianne asked. Jeremy returned Stella to the floor and Stella yelled in her excitement, "Uncle Jeremy! Will you come out to the beach with me and Mommy? We're going to dig and build a sandcastle."

Jeremy turned toward her. "I'd love to, sweetheart. But you and Mommy go on out. I'll meet you out there after I talk to your daddy about something."

After they left, Jeremy walked over to Tom. "You okay, Tom?"

"What do you think?"

"I think you're probably a little worked up about everything that's been going on around here. Am I right?"

Tom rolled his eyes. "Again. What do you think?"

Jeremy looked to the floor, considering. "I think you're thinking that the fire wouldn't have happened if it weren't for me. And of course, you're right. Slotky was going after me, pure and simple. I just didn't know who was behind it, or I would've stopped him."

"You put my family in danger. The entire place could've gone up in flames."

"You're right about that. But the minute they put the fire out, I moved all remaining stock out of here. The last thing I wanted to do was put you or anyone else at the Inn in danger."

A streak of light shot through Tom's head and he stepped closer to Jeremy, just inches away from his face now, leaning in. "But you did put someone at the Inn in danger, didn't you?"

Jeremy's mouth dropped, his eyes went wide. "Stella?"

"That's right. That old man befriended her, Jeremy. Talked with her, played with her, gave her a gift. She believed in him. What the hell? What was my innocent five-year-old supposed to think when a man her grandpa's age is showering attention on her? Is she supposed to be suspicious and think he's going to harm her?"

"No, no, of course not."

"But you exposed her to this maniac. You. So it was *you* who put her in danger."

Jeremy looked down at his shoes. His torment flickered across his face. He cleared his throat and his face flushed. "I, I'm sorry. I didn't mean for any of this to happen. Obviously.

You have to know that, Tom. I'd never want any harm to come to Stella. I'd protect her with my life."

"Well, despite the bad forces that you exposed her to, it appears she's going to make a full recovery. But you'll forgive me if I don't welcome you back into her life, and our Inn with open arms." He stepped back a few paces. "I have to protect what's mine."

Jeremy stared at him for a long moment. Then he ran his hands through his hair, his hands appearing to operate with a mind of their own. He dropped them to his side and nodded. "Are you saying ... I'm not welcome here, Tom?"

"If you were in my shoes, what would you do?"

Jeremy let out a big breath, gave him one last gaze, and walked out the door.

Chapter Five

The next few days epitomized the joy and beauty of life on the beach. One day blended seamlessly into the next, filled with unfettered moments of happiness and relief with Stella. She could get used to this, Marianne decided. Her dad and Leslie were still coming over and taking over the tasks she'd normally be responsible for, leaving her all kinds of free time with her daughter. Uninterrupted time to observe Stella and make her own determination of her mental state. She searched for signs that Stella was in distress. Any indication that she was suffering emotionally from her terrifying ordeal.

She wasn't a psychologist or a therapist, but Marianne wasn't seeing a thing. No nightmares marred the peaceful darkness of Stella's bedroom. No uncomfortable questions for she and Tom to address. No hesitation when she left her parents' side. No tears that popped up inexplicably. No, she showed every indication of being the same well-adjusted five-year-old that she was before the abduction.

But that couldn't possibly be true. Could it?

Could their family have dodged a bullet like this? Did Stella have no remnant aftereffects from being kidnapped, using her wits to escape a madman, only to find herself alone in the woods to fend for herself?

Or, if she were a better mother, would she recognize hidden signs that her daughter needed help? Signs that if missed now, would only grow more disastrous later when they emerged.

Marianne sighed and vowed to quit making herself crazy. *God, help me deal with this. Help me accept that my Stella may be fine. Help me accept that she may not. But let me enjoy each precious moment, as it comes.*

She looked up as a shadow passed over her. Leslie stood beside her, blocking the sun from her eyes. She put her hand on the top of her floppy beach hat and smiled up at her. "Hi. Let me pull a chair up for you."

"No, you relax. I got it." Leslie looked around, found a wooden beach chair a short distance away and dragged it over. Marianne admired the older woman's grace as she reclined. The woman reeked of class. Petite, fit, blonde and possessing a classic beauty, she'd always reminded Marianne of a young Doris Day, except she was quintessentially modern.

Leslie was the total opposite of Marianne.

Tall, buxom, still carrying at least ten pounds of "baby weight," despite the fact that her baby had been around for half a decade. Hair that defied a color description, other than just "brown." Not chestnut or russet or caramel. And graceful was the last word people would think to describe her. In fact, she'd had more than her share of clumsy moments.

"How's she doing?" Leslie asked, looking over at Stella who was, of course, digging in the sand. A bunch of it covered her elbows and knees, and enough of it coated her hands that if she chose that moment to rub her eyes, disaster would strike.

"Unbelievably good."

"Great." Leslie smiled. Marianne paused a second, wondering if she should voice her doom and gloom, then changed her mind, looked away.

"What?" Leslie asked, always alert.

Marianne shrugged. "I just hope I'm not missing anything I shouldn't be."

Leslie watched Stella busily fill a plastic bucket, then rise and walk to the water's edge. "It's normal to want to help our children through their hard times. Nothing's going to happen on a schedule. She may or may not have aftereffects. And they may not come right away. The important thing is, you're doing all the right things. You've taken her to a therapist. You have more sessions coming up. She's a professional and will know what questions to ask. You're spending time with Stella, and she knows how much you love her." Leslie patted her on the shoulder. "Try not to worry."

Marianne sighed. "I'm just so afraid that this will be the event that turns out to be the start of all the troubles in her life. In our lives."

Leslie nodded. "You can't live in fear that bad things will happen to you. You need to live your life and be thankful for the good, and pray for help with the bad. Prayer helps, you know."

Marianne nodded. "Yeah," she started, and then looked up. Stella stood ankle-high in the water with her bucket, filling it with tidewater. As Marianne watched, a wave knocked her off-balance. Stella stumbled a step or two, then fell in the water. Marianne gasped and stood, ran across the sand. A couple with gray hair, walking barefoot, approached Stella and held out a hand to steady her. Marianne yelled, "Stella! I'm here, baby."

The older couple looked up, alarmed, looked back at her little girl who was struggling to get to her feet. Marianne raced past them, scrambled into the water, reached down and lifted her up, splashes of salt water going everywhere and landing on the couple. "I've got her. I'm here. Don't touch her, please."

Marianne barely recognized her own frantic voice, and her heart raced. She regretted the expressions she'd put on their faces, and sincerely hoped they weren't guests of the Seaside Inn; she didn't believe they were. Maybe they were staying at a neighboring Inn, or one of the rental houses down the beach. They probably thought she was crazy, and her reaction completely unwarranted.

But they had no idea. They couldn't know what they'd been through.

"Mommy," Stella whimpered.

"You're okay, baby. Mommy's here." She squeezed Stella tight, holding the girl's head against her shoulder.

"Mom! Let me go." Stella wrenched herself from her grasp and Marianne lowered her carefully to the sand. Stella shot her a look, a mix between confused and irritated, picked up her bucket and trekked back to her castle.

Her arms were shaking and her head pulsed. A soft hand on her shoulder, a soft voice in her ear. It was Leslie. "You okay, sweetie?"

Marianne drew a shaky breath. "That was probably over the top, and I'm afraid I was extremely rude to that poor couple who were just trying to help."

Leslie gave a sad little smile. She didn't agree, but she didn't disagree either. "Next time you go see that therapist, you might want to mention to her how you're feeling."

It was such a gentle little nudge, Marianne couldn't help laughing. "You think?"

Leslie nodded, smiling. "Can't hurt!"

* * *

The peaceful solitude of the darkened Inn helped her anxieties to fade, for the moment, anyway. Marianne and Tom sat in an abandoned corner of the dining room, enjoying glasses of Pinot Grigio. Marianne lifted her legs and rested her stockinged feet in his lap. He gave her an exaggerated eyeroll, then used one hand to massage them.

"Ahhhh," she moaned. "One of the perks of being married to you."

He snorted. "Is that one towards the top or bottom of the list?"

She smiled, eyes closed. "Right in the middle."

After a few moments of blissful quiet, she told him about her episode with Stella and the older couple in the water.

"Marianne," he began, his determination to control his anger during this moment of togetherness clear, even to her ears. "You've done it again. This really surprises me about you. I've never seen you this out of control with Stella before."

She took a ragged breath, her stomach clenching and tears threatening her eyes. "You interrupted me before I could tell you — I know I was wrong. In fact, I told Leslie I knew I handled it all wrong. I didn't stop and think, I just reacted. I'm hyper-alert to perceived danger now."

He sighed and shook his head. "It's maternal instinct, but you really need to get control over these cases where you fly off the handle unreasonably. You just end up scaring Stella, and that's the last thing she needs."

Marianne nodded. "And I was unintentionally rude to that poor couple. They were just trying to help, and a crazy mama comes flying in, chasing them away. Bad advertising for the Inn, at the very least."

Tom shrugged. "I'm not worried about that. My worry is for Stella. You've got to get a grip on your emotions, Marianne." His massaging increased in intensity. "Everything we do, Stella is watching. She's a very smart child, an observant child. Not only have *we* never been through a kidnapping before, but let's not forget *she* never has either. She has no idea how to react. She's taking her cue from us. If we freak out and go crazy, so will she. And that's not healthy."

Marianne sighed. "You're right..."

"She seems to have taken this thing in stride. She wasn't hurt, she was found quickly, she's safe. Let's not screw that up by our emotional over-reactions."

Marianne opened her eyes and directed them at his. "When you say 'our,' you mean 'my,' don't you?"

"Well, yeah. Don't you think I have crazy paternal instincts urging me to protect our child? Go hunt down that guy and make him pay? But I control them. I have to act in a way that is right for Stella. And you do too."

His massaging had crossed the border into downright painful, so she pulled her feet away. "Okay."

"Just stop and think before you act. You're a reasonable person. Don't let instinct take over. You know what you have to do. You have to make a safe home for Stella. Now, do it."

She nodded. Time to put on her big girl hat and be a mom again. The adult who knew what she was doing. The one in charge.

She cleared her throat and savored another sip of wine. "I think Leslie needs to get back to work. And I'm sure my dad's put off enough of his jobs too. Do you think we're ready to take over the responsibilities of the Inn?"

He gave a firm nod. "Yep. We'll thank them for their help and take over again tomorrow."

"Why don't I invite them over for dinner tomorrow night? I think we're having shrimp scampi. I can reserve a big table and have a family celebration."

Tom raised his eyebrows. "A big table? Just for us, Hank and Leslie?"

"I was thinking Jeremy and Emma too. And maybe I'll reach out to some of the volunteer rescuers we know personally. Make it a 'thank you' dinner for everyone who helped bring our Stella back."

Tom straightened in his chair and his face crushed into disapproval. "I don't know about that, Marianne."

"Why not?"

He paused for just a moment too long. "It might be hard on Stella seeing all those people again."

She frowned. "What do you mean, it would bring back bad memories?"

"Yeah."

She shook her head. "I'm confused. Didn't you just lecture me about not being overly protective of her? To get life back to normal? Stella loves parties. She loves big family dinners. I think this would be just what she'd want."

She knew him well enough to know when he was biting his tongue. "What? You really don't want to host a thank you dinner for all the folks who helped us with Stella?"

His lips tightened, like they were holding in words.

"What is it, Tom? You're worried about something, but it's not how Stella would react to a fun dinner in her honor."

He thought one more moment, then shook his head. "No, you're right. Go ahead and plan it. You invite the folks, I'll talk to Toby tomorrow about the menu."

"How's seven?" she asked. By then, the Inn guests would be done with their dinners, and would have wandered out of the dining room, leaving more open space for their celebration. And less people to disturb if they got loud.

He nodded.

She smiled, a sense of giddiness invading her. "Great. I feel good about this." This would help them get back to normal. She and Tom were a couple who loved to entertain. And since they'd bought the Inn, they had plenty of space for it. Stella was raised with people and friends all around her. Perfect remedy. She stood and leaned over Tom's head, landing a kiss on top of it. "I'll get busy with phone calls before it gets too late."

* * *

It was shortly after 9:30 when she called her brother.

"Marianne? What's wrong?"

She chuckled. She couldn't blame him for assuming disaster. "No, no, nothing. I'm sorry for the late call, but Tom and I just decided. We want to have a little party tomorrow night. We want to invite everyone who helped search for Stella. I mean, those ones we know and are personally acquainted with."

"Oh," he breathed, and she could hear the relief in his voice.

"I'm sure you can remember more names of volunteers than I can."

"Yeah, I suppose so." They brainstormed and after ten minutes, Marianne had compiled a list of at least a dozen. With spouses and significant others, if everyone could attend, they'd have a real hoe-down.

"That's nice of you, Marianne. Those folks give up their personal time, in addition to work time and all, and tromp around looking for lost people. They don't always get thanked. I'm sure they'll really appreciate it."

"Tom's working with Toby to make sure we have a great dinner. We're setting it for seven o'clock. I assume you're available?"

Jeremy went silent. "Me?"

Marianne laughed. "Of course, you. You and Emma were the ones who found her. You're the guests of honor!"

Another pause. "Did you say Tom approved this party?"

Marianne frowned. "Well, he did eventually. Why do you ask?"

"He didn't like the idea originally?"

Her brother was hemming and she wanted to know why. Now. "He thought maybe it would stir up bad memories for Stella. He's just being protective. But he's wrong. This will be wonderful for Stella and remind her how much everyone loves her." She wrapped the curly-que phone cord around her finger from the old-fashioned phone behind the guest desk in the lobby. "What's on your mind, Jeremy? Why are you worried about what Tom thinks?"

"No, nothing. It's a great idea, sis, but unfortunately, Emma and I can't make it tomorrow night. We've got plans."

"Ohhh," Marianne groaned, disappointed. "How about Monday night then?"

"Don't change your plans for us."

"No, it's okay. You two have to be there. You guys found her. It's the whole point of the dinner. I'd be happy to adjust the date of the party around your schedule."

Jeremy let out a breath of air.

"There's something you're not telling me. Why don't you just come clean?"

Jeremy chuckled, but to Marianne's ears it sounded nervous and forced. "You're paranoid, sis. Listen, you go ahead and plan for tomorrow night and we'll do our best to be there."

"It won't be the same without you."

"Thanks, I appreciate that."

Chapter Six

The next evening, the Inn glistened from the last-minute scrubbing Marianne had given it. Toby had outdone himself with not only the earlier dinner for the Inn guests, but the spur-of-the-moment dinner party for what turned out to be thirty-five guests.

Marianne had telephoned all the search and rescue volunteers Jeremy had told her about, and happily, the majority were free. Marianne worked with Stella during the day to craft little party favors for each guest — a conch shell filled with sand and a candle, the shell straight from the collection Marianne kept of all the treasures she and Stella had picked up straight from the beach on morning walks.

"Everyone coming for dinner tonight helped look for you, and helped bring you home safely," she explained to Stella. The little girl smiled and nodded as she worked beside her mom on the creations.

At seven, the Inn's dining room filled up with grateful, hungry people, thrilled about the happy ending. Marianne imagined not all of their volunteer searches ended as well as this one had.

The tables filled and Tom got on the microphone and said, "Thank you so much for joining us tonight. And more than anything, thank you for your volunteer hours, searching for our daughter Stella last week. It was easily the most terrifying night of our lives, but because of you all, she was safely found and brought home. Stella?"

Stella walked over to her dad, who lifted her up onto his shoulders. She waved and the room exploded in a round of applause. Stella smiled and giggled.

Marianne scanned the people in the room. Although Tom was thanking everyone for bringing her home safely, the two people who found her and actually brought her home, were glaringly absent. A stab of disappointment pierced her heart. Where was Jeremy? And what could he possibly have going on tonight that was more important than this? What was it that he couldn't miss?

Maybe he was just running behind schedule. If that was the case, she was sorry he'd missed Tom's speech, but at least he'd still be here for dinner. She pulled out her cell phone and called him. The phone rang three times, then went to his voicemail. She waited for it to end, then said, "Jeremy, you should be here. Tom just thanked everyone for bringing Stella home safely. You're missing this. Hope to see you soon."

Tom and Marianne helped the normal Inn wait staff in bringing out steaming plates of fresh shrimp scampi over rice, spinach salad and warm rolls to all the tables. Although Leslie insisted on helping, Marianne forced her to sit and enjoy her meal like the honored guest she was. Hank chuckled and patted his bride's hand.

Stella loved being the center of attention, and Marianne smiled watching her soak in the love and affection from all the folks who came over to their table to talk. She glanced at Tom. He didn't seem in the least worried or anxious about the dinner anymore. She supposed he could see firsthand that Stella was blossoming.

Homemade cheesecake with strawberry sauce ended the meal, along with coffee and cream. Marianne helped pass them all out, then sat to enjoy her own. Stella yawned and toyed at hers with a fork, then pushed it away.

"What's the matter, honey?"

"I don't like this," she said.

"Have you ever tried it?"

She shook her head.

Marianne scooped a tiny bite on her fork and directed it to Stella, but she shook her head. Poor little thing was tired out and getting grumpy. "That's okay, sweetie, you don't have to eat it."

"I want dessert, though!" she moaned.

Marianne looked around. Last thing she needed was an emotional meltdown courtesy of the guest of honor. "We have vanilla ice cream. Do you want that?"

Stella's eyes lit up. "Ice cream!"

Marianne pushed her chair back. "Okay, I'll get it for you."

"But not vanilla."

Marianne swung her head back. "That's the only flavor we have, honey."

Stella stuck her bottom lip out. "Chocolate peanut butter cup."

"We don't have that."

Stella rolled her eyes and flung her body forward so fast she bumped her head on the table.

Marianne never intentionally spoiled her child, however, she knew the beauty of picking her battles. If a quick trip to the grocery store would stop an inevitable over-tired temper tantrum, she'd rather pick the lesser of two evils. Stella sat upright, tears in her eyes. Marianne patted her hand. "All right, listen. I will go get you chocolate peanut butter cup ice cream, and you will continue to be a polite, happy little girl, you got me?"

Stella pulled herself together and delivered a brave nod.

Marianne glanced around the crowded dining room and found Tom a few tables away, talking. She stole over in his direction and clued him in on her sudden need to visit the grocery store. He frowned but nodded. "I'll keep an eye on her."

A few minutes later she was driving to the grocery store. It didn't take long — nothing on Pawleys Island took long to reach. From tip to tip, it covered three miles, and only a quarter of a mile wide. Her car was a convenience, but certainly not a requirement here on the island.

She pulled into the Piggly Wiggly parking lot, grabbed her purse and trotted through the glass doors. She headed straight toward the freezer section and took only a moment to locate Stella's favorite flavor. She grabbed it and turned, single-minded in her goal. She could return and slide a bowl of scooped ice cream in front of Stella not ten minutes after she left. She wasn't counting on colliding with someone on her way to the same freezer. She dropped her carton. Apologizing for her clumsiness, she watched the tube-like container roll away on the floor. Marianne darted after it, bent and retrieved it before connecting eyes with her victim.

"I'm so sorr …," she came to a halt mid-sentence. "Emma!"

Marianne had to hand it to her — her brother's girlfriend managed to pop a happy smile on her face, even as she was rubbing her forehead from the *conk* it received against the freezer door. "Oh, hi Marianne."

"I'm so sorry I ran into you. I wasn't watching. I was so excited to find this flavor. It was exactly what I needed." She held up the carton with diminishing glee.

Emma peered at the packaging. "Oh my, that does sound good. I think that would be worth a bump on the head."

Marianne groaned. "I feel so awful. I know we haven't spent much time together. I'm really not this dangerous all the time."

Emma laughed. "No, not at all. Don't be silly."

"Stella's a little overstimulated from being the center of attention all night, and although I'm sure a sugar overload is the opposite of what she needs right now, I didn't want to deal with the meltdown that was ensuing when she looked at her cheesecake."

Emma furrowed her brow, looking very much like a young woman who was trying to follow the train of thought but having absolutely no luck.

Marianne sighed. "Listen to me babble." She gave her head a brisk shake to try to clear it. "Never mind. What are you doing on Pawleys tonight?" Emma lived in Myrtle Beach, which, although not far, was much better stocked with grocery stores than their little island.

Emma smiled. "Hanging out with Jeremy tonight. He made us burgers on the grill, and we both had a little sweet tooth. So I offered to run out for ice cream."

Marianne blinked, stared at the girl's pretty face and massive mound of curly brown hair. "Tonight? You and Jeremy are hanging out at his house tonight?"

Emma nodded happily.

"Did you have plans earlier?" Her ears were starting to pound with the implication of what she was hearing. Jeremy had told Marianne he couldn't come to Stella's party because he and Emma had plans. Plans they couldn't break to come to Stella's party. But no, according to Emma, they'd been hanging out at his house eating hamburgers.

What the heck?

Emma shook her head, looking a little uncertain.

"Emma, let me ask you something. Did Jeremy mention Stella's party tonight?"

"Stella? No. No, he didn't."

The ice cream carton she had tucked under her arm was causing her skin to turn numb. She pulled it out, shifted it to her other hand. "Well, you have a nice night now." She took off, only vaguely regretting the look of complete confusion on the girl's face.

* * *

The guests were gone. Stella was in bed, sound asleep after enjoying her bowl of specially ordered ice cream, the kitchen was clean enough that Marianne could retire and finish putting all the clean dishes away tomorrow. She and Tom were in the bathroom, going through their bedtime routine.

"I ran into Emma Slotky in the Piggly Wiggly tonight."

She glanced over at her husband. He was brushing his teeth, stopped momentarily, then shook his head, pointing at his ear. He mumbled something, leaned in and spit. "Couldn't hear you. What?"

"I said, I ran into Emma Slotky in the Piggly Wiggly tonight while I was getting Stella's ice cream."

His expression tightened. He was quiet a moment, then stuck the toothbrush back in his mouth, brushing slowly. His eyes squinted. "Who?"

Marianne scoffed. "What do you mean, who? You know who Emma Slotky is."

"Oh," he said, awareness dawning. "Jeremy's girl?"

"Of course."

"Ah. That's nice. Did you talk to her?"

Marianne sighed and gave his arm a gentle but well-deserved punch. "Yes, of course I talked to her, and no, it's *not* nice that I saw her there. Remember Jeremy told me that he and Emma had plans they couldn't easily break, and that's why they couldn't come to Stella's party tonight. But when I talked to Emma, she said they had just grilled hamburgers at his house, and he'd never even mentioned the party to her."

Tom spit again, rinsed out his mouth and the brush, and placed it carefully back in the stand. He started to walk toward the door and Marianne reached out and grabbed the tie belt of his bathrobe. "Don't you think that's rather odd, Tom?"

Tom turned and shrugged. "No, not really."

Marianne frowned. "No? Why not?"

"They're a young couple, just getting to know each other. Spending an evening surrounded by people, when they could be home alone together, isn't all that odd. In my opinion. Is all I'm saying."

Marianne shook her head. "Jeremy is big into family. I don't buy it."

Tom pulled her close and landed his lips on hers. He took her by surprise and she gasped. Then pulse racing, finished the kiss unrushed. He pulled back first. "Don't you remember when our favorite thing to do was to spend the evening home alone together?" He winked and started out the door again.

Marianne followed. "Regardless, that's rude to receive an invitation, then make up a lie about not accepting it."

"Well, Jeremy's been out of circulation for a while, Marianne. Maybe he's not up on social etiquette."

"That's not it. This is common sense."

"Seriously, he was incarcerated for a decade. Wouldn't you forget about a lot of daily niceties when you were just trying to survive for ten years?"

Marianne took her robe off, hung it over the easy chair near the bed. "Still, it's just not like Jeremy." She picked up the phone from the bedside table and slid under the covers. She had just poked at the first number when Tom's alarmed voice stopped her.

"What are you doing?"

She looked up at him, wide-eyed. "Calling Jeremy."

"No, no, that's not a good idea."

She studied him for a moment. He'd never shown any interest or concern about when she called her brother. Why did he care now? "Why?"

Tom's smile seemed a little too forced. "Give the guy a break. He's got a young lady. Give them some privacy."

Marianne looked back at the phone. "Nah, we're pretty close, Tom. I caught him in a lie, and I want to find out why." She stabbed at a few buttons before Tom reached over and swiped the phone away.

"At least do it tomorrow. It's late. I have plans for the two of us. Plans that just involve you and me. No adorable little five-year-old girl. No brother and whether he lied to you or not. No roomful of guests."

His voice was low and gravelly in that way that it always got when he wanted some intimacy. Which hadn't been all that often lately. They were way too busy with the business, with Stella, and of course, recently, with all the strange happenings at the Inn, courtesy of Emma's father. The last thing she wanted to do was push him off.

She loved her husband and savored their private time together. He slid into the bed beside her and took her into his arms. A few moments into their kiss, her concerns fled and the only thing on her mind was him.

Chapter Seven

The next morning, life got back to normal. Their schedule resumed. No more help running the Inn from Leslie and Hank. Every year throughout February and March, the retired snowbirds checked out and went home after spending a heavenly four, six or eight weeks at the Inn. Today, one room occupied by guests for the last two months was being vacated, and another couple was moving in for a week.

Marianne tapped on the computer keyboard as the lovely white-haired couple handed her their credit card to pay for the last incidentals of their stay. Mrs. Broomstead sighed and patted Marianne's hand. "We had such a wonderful time. Thank you for your hospitality."

"We were so happy to have you. We'd love to welcome you back next year. In fact, would you like to put a hold on a room for next year?"

The two looked at each other and chuckled. "We were talking about this last night. We've loved it here, but this is our first extended winter stay. We feel like we need to experiment. Sample several areas before we settle on just one."

Mr. Broomstead tucked the card back into his wallet. "Maybe try the Outer Banks in North Carolina next year. Or venture into Florida."

Marianne handed him the credit card receipt to sign. "I understand. But we'll miss you."

Mrs. B replied, "It's such a beautiful place, Pawleys. But oh my, you've had some scary times this winter, haven't you? Between the fire, and the kidnapping and getting your sweet little daughter back."

Marianne looked up at her while her husband finished the transaction. "We're getting our feet back on the ground. Stella is doing wonderfully."

The older lady nodded.

"But let me ask you, is that part of the reason you're not returning next year? You're worried about the troubles we've been having?"

"Oh no, dear, no. Not at all."

"Although," Mr. B said, "you're very lucky that fire didn't spread and cause major damage. If your place had burned down, or injured, or God forbid, killed any of your guests, you'd be in a heap of trouble, wouldn't you?"

Marianne felt her shoulders shudder. "Yes, you're right about that. But God was looking over us all, that's for sure."

Marianne called for Tom, who carried the couple's luggage out to the car. When he returned back inside, she motioned him over. "Tom, the Broomsteads aren't coming back next year. I think it's because of the fire and the kidnapping."

Tom shook his head. "They told me they want to try other places before they settle on going to the same place every year."

Marianne came out from behind the guest desk. "They told me that too, but I think the real reason is the trouble we had this year. It's chasing business away."

Tom took a glance around the room. "We don't know that. And we don't want to talk about it in front of the guests. Let's do a quiet survey of the rest of the folks who check out over the next few weeks. We'll offer them a discount if they reserve for next year and put a deposit down. If they decline, we'll politely ask them why. Let's not jump to any conclusions until we have a little more data."

Marianne shook out her trembling hands. Tom was so good at this. His plan was logical and made sense. Gathering data was infinitely better than getting irrationally nervous. She squeezed one of his hands, leaned in for a kiss on his cheek.

"I'll get busy with cleaning the Broomsteads' room. The new guests will be here this afternoon."

Several hours later, Marianne was done deep-cleaning the room, and had moved on to working on payroll for the few paid employees of the Inn. She popped her head up and reached for her cell phone. She'd been busy and had never called Jeremy about his absence last night. She sighed when it went to his voicemail, waited for the beep and said, "Jeremy, it's your sister. I need to talk to you about the party last night. Give me a call when you get this and have a moment to talk."

* * *

A few days later, it was time for Stella's second therapist appointment. Marianne attached her daughter's seat belt and drove over to Stephanie Reynolds' office. After a short wait, the therapist came to the waiting room to welcome them. "How's everything going?"

Marianne smiled. "Stella's doing great. I'm starting to calm down a little bit. I think."

"Glad to hear it. We'll talk more about your feelings, and your husband's, when you come in for your family session. Meanwhile, take one day at a time and acknowledge the positive."

"Good advice."

Stephanie invited Stella into her office and closed the door.

Marianne selected a short stack of magazines to keep herself busy. But ten minutes into reading about Angelina and Brad and their huge family, her thoughts wandered to the decline of their returning guests. Although no one had checked out since the Broomsteads, she recalled two snowbird couples who had checked out the week before, and wouldn't commit to a return visit. Winters were a tough season for an ocean front inn on the coast of South Carolina. Temperatures didn't stay warm enough for swimming in the ocean, or even for playing golf in the worst winter months, as they did in southern Florida. Although a barefoot walk on the beach bundled up in a sweatshirt and jacket was heavenly to some, other guests wanted to soak in the sun, even in January or February.

As innkeepers, it was their priority to present their guests with such a wonderful stay that they wanted to come back year after year. And they needed to fill at least half, but better yet, two thirds of their guest rooms year-round in order to meet their expenses and stay profitable.

She sat in the silence of the waiting room and her pulse started to race with worry. She and Tom were totally committed to the Inn as their family income. If it failed, they would be in trouble. Their entire lives would have to change. Tom would have to find a new job. Depending on his income, Marianne would need to find one too, and Stella

would have to spend her afternoons in daycare after school. And since the Inn was their home as well, they'd have to sell the place, probably at a loss, and find a new home. And what were the chances they'd find two jobs and a new home in tiny Pawleys Island? They'd have to leave.

But where? Myrtle Beach? Nearby Hilton Head Island? Or, away from the beach altogether.

When Stella finished her appointment with Stephanie and returned to the waiting room, Marianne had worked herself up into such a nervous state that she had to fake a casual "good-bye" to the therapist. Her hands shook, her breath raced, her heart pounded. Sitting in the car, she took a moment to calm herself before starting the engine. It wasn't safe to drive like this. She closed her eyes until Stella got suspicious with their inactivity and asked, "Mama? What are we doing? What are we waiting for?" Marianne said a silent prayer, *Dear Father, please help me, guide me, show me what's right for me and my family. I turn my worries over to you, Father. Show me what to do and help me to find peace.*

She opened her eyes and adjusted her shoulders to get the tension out. She put a smile on her face and turned to look at Stella in the back seat. "Everything's fine, sweetie. We'll go home now. How was your appointment with Stephanie?"

As Stella regaled her with stories of what she remembered from her appointment, Marianne drove them both home.

* * *

Tom returned his sand rake to the utility shed behind the Inn, and dumped his trash. One of the features of the Seaside Inn that attracted guests was the clean white sand beach. The expanse connecting the Inn to the ocean, he considered their private real estate, even if the town of Pawleys Island didn't necessarily agree. And one benefit to guests of a private beach was that it was immaculately manicured. Each morning, he took an early morning beach walk, holding his garbage bag, and he would clean up the sand of remnants of vicious battles between sea animals overnight. Halves of horseshoe crabs, just the crisp skeletal remains, the interior meat scavenged by sea animals of unknown sort. Jellyfish, clear and gelatinous, coated with sand, now lay lifeless, having been washed up onto shore. And seaweed — all size, shape and manner of slimy green seaweed, which, although a member of God's nature, were unpleasant for swimmers to brush against underwater, making them scream and kick until they realize it's nothing dangerous.

One by one, each morning, into the plastic bag they'd go. When the whole expanse of beach behind the Inn was cleared of natural rubbish, Tom would rake the sand back to a flat, even surface. He knew the guests appreciated it, but he was doing it for selfish reasons as well. He loved this method of starting his day. For six years now, it was his routine. Oh, so much better than showering, dressing in a suit, and racing to the office, where he'd spend all day on the phone and doing paperwork.

He looked up to the sky with a silent *thank you* to the Lord for this life he and Marianne and formed.

His work done for the moment, he set off to his right and walked, for exercise, sure, but more for his mind than body. A solitary walk along the water's edge, the sound of the waves moving continuously in and out, did wonders for working through a problem.

And his biggest problem now was … his family. Marianne and Stella were his world, the most important people in his life. He would do whatever he had to, to keep them safe. What had happened to Stella was unforgiveable. And completely avoidable. He'd never be caught unaware again. In his mind, the solution was clear: Jeremy.

Jeremy was at the center of all the problems they'd experienced over the last few months. Thank God it all turned out okay. But it was his job to make sure he never allowed anything to harm Stella again.

That was an easy fix. Disband from Jeremy. That simple.

Let Jeremy live his own life, awa from Tom's. If he wanted to fall in love with the daughter of the crazy man who kidnapped Stella, that was Jeremy's business. Tom didn't care enough to discourage him. But let Jeremy ride his own runaway train. He didn't need to drag Tom and his family along.

And there lied the problem. Marianne.

Ever since he and Marianne had dated, he knew about her brother who was away at prison. He knew the whole story. He'd even accompanied Marianne to visit him once or twice. They got married and Jeremy wasn't there. They bought the Inn and Jeremy wasn't there. They had Stella and Jeremy wasn't there. Life had gone on without Jeremy, and life was good.

But when Jeremy was released in August, he saw something new in Marianne. A maternal instinct, some kind of over-the-top dedication to her rehabilitated brother that surprised him. Sure, Marianne was always the type to give stray animals a home and invite lonely people over for dinner. It was part of who she was, why he loved her so much. He expected her to welcome Jeremy back home, make him feel part of the family.

What he didn't expect was the extravagance with which she did it.

She gave him a place to live — a room in their Inn for free until he could get other living arrangements made. She fed him — from their dining room, for free, not only while he lived here, but even after he moved out. She advertised his furniture business in the Inn's great room. She gave him marketing ideas and created full-color materials for him. She didn't think twice about encouraging their daughter to idolize her Uncle Jeremy.

And that's where he and she parted in their thinking.

If she hadn't pulled Jeremy so deeply into their lives after his return from prison, Stella wouldn't have been kidnapped. Period.

And therefore, Jeremy will no longer be a part of their lives. Jeremy seemed to accept Tom's decision as head of the household. He didn't show up and disrupt Stella's rescue party. Now, Tom's challenge was to make Marianne see his way of thinking.

His knees ached with the hike through the sand, and he looked up and took note of his location. He smirked. In his self-absorbed thoughts, he'd hiked at least two miles. His breath came in pants. Better turn around and head home.

Moving at a more leisurely pace now, he planned how he would tell Marianne that for the safety of their family and especially their daughter, her brother was no longer welcome in their Inn. He couldn't stop him from coming to family occasions outside of their home, but dang it, he was the head of this family. And he had every right to make and enforce his own rules.

Because once upon a time, he wasn't the one in charge, his dad was. And his dad didn't set and enforce the rules.

And the family went through hell because of it. He was determined not to inherit his father's weakness. He would run his family the way he felt was right.

God help him.

Chapter Eight

Marianne set out with the grocery list in hand for the next few days. Although they'd hired cooks to prepare all the meals, she did the shopping for the ingredients. She enjoyed the search, and usually spread her purchases over several stores, both on the island and over the bridge on the mainland. She and Tom had a strategy when they'd started, hiring high-quality chefs, and paying them more than they thought they could afford. They wanted the Seaside Inn to be known for their excellent all-inclusive meals, in addition to the best stretch of beach, and of course, the southern hospitality.

But halfway to the first grocery store, she changed her route. Instead, she turned to the north and drove just a few miles to her brother's new warehouse/storefront. It wasn't open to the public yet, but would be eventually. Meanwhile, he was busy replacing furniture inventory that had gotten destroyed by Mr. Slotky, and preparing for a Grand Opening.

As she pulled up to the strip mall storefront, she couldn't help but think that the fire at their storage shed had resulted in one positive thing. Jeremy needed a warehouse of his own if he were going to dream big with his business. When he built custom furniture in his backyard on a tarp thrown on the grass, it was a hobby. When he moved his finished inventory to the storage shed at the Inn, it was a step toward considering it a business. Now, he couldn't deny it was a business — he'd invested in the monthly rental. God works in mysterious ways sometimes.

She stepped out of the car and walked up to the plate-glass window. She peered in and thought she detected movement towards the back. She went to the door and rapped on it loudly with her knuckles.

After a brief wait, Jeremy opened the door, immediately looking sheepish. "Hey, sis." He pulled her into a hug, resting his forehead on her shoulder.

"Jeremy, what is up with you?" She cringed when she heard the critical tone in her own voice, knowing that he of course had detected it as well.

He pulled back from her and shrugged. "Want to come in?"

She nodded and followed him in. He locked the door behind them, and she took in the immensity of his new space. "Wow," she breathed. "You have a ton of room here, don't you?"

"Sure do. I'm working night and day to fill it. Emma is helping me plan a Grand Opening but I want to make sure I have plenty to display."

Marianne took a few steps in. When his stock had been stuffed into her storage shed, tables and bookcases were stacked on top of each other to fit into the small space. Here, there was room for everything. Plenty of room to showcase the beautiful oak and cedar and pine creations that Jeremy was becoming known for. Although he'd taken a hit to his stock due to the recent troubles, he'd been busy replacing. At least twenty pieces were scattered around the room.

"You seem to have a lot right now."

"No, not enough. Many of these I've restored from the fire and the water damage, so I'll price those at a discount. I need to put my best foot forward for the Grand Opening. Impress the heck out of people and give them a reason to come back."

His words made her smile with pride. Her big brother had been through adversity, but was working to get back on track. He was a hard worker, determined to make his own way.

A Bible verse jumped into her mind. "Humble yourself before the Lord and He will lift you up." This described Jeremy, to a tee. A humble man working hard, not expecting any handouts. And she couldn't wait until the Lord lifted him up in His glory.

Jeremy gave her an odd look. "What, sis?"

She gave her head a swift shake, momentarily speechless with the advent of tears pricking her eyes. "Nothing. Just proud of you."

He frowned, his forehead creased with confusion. "Why on earth would you be proud of me?"

She took a few steps closer to him and brushed his elbow with her hand. Then she gestured to the open space around them. "This. This is a huge step, an investment in your business, your future success. You're making all your dreams come true. You're putting your talents to work to support yourself. You're working hard and doing all the right things."

He blinked, dipped his head. "It never ceases to amaze me how generous you are, sis. Your faith in me is largely unfounded; you do realize that, don't you?"

"That's not true."

"It is. I've given you no reason to have such great faith in me. I'm a screw-up and caused major problems for my family, including you. And I don't know exactly how to handle your praise and support."

"That's ridic …" Her cell phone rang and she stopped to dig it out of her purse. "Oh, it's Tom. Hold on."

Jeremy turned away.

"Hey honey. I'm on my way to the store …"

"Yes, I wasn't sure when you'd be back, but I had an idea while on the beach this morning. How about a night out, just the two of us?"

"Two? What about Stella?"

"She'll be fine without us for a few hours. We'll take her over to Hank and Leslie's. How about it?"

Being separated from Stella for any reason was unappetizing these days. But it would be nice for her to spend time with her grandparents. Her dad and Leslie would enjoy it as well. And how often did her husband, as much as she loved him, get his mind off the business and onto her? That kind of thoughtfulness was something she should encourage, not discourage.

"Well, okay, sure. I'll get dressed up and we'll enjoy some alone time."

"That's my girl. Great. I'll see you when you get back."

She hung up, smiling despite her anxieties. It would be good for them to focus on their relationship for a change. Life, with all its responsibilities, consumed them both and they rarely put intentional focus on each other.

When she turned back to Jeremy, he'd moved over to a long farm-style kitchen table, and was running his fingers over the surface. "By the way, there was a reason I came over here today. I've been trying to get a hold of you for several days."

"Oh, really?" he mumbled.

"Didn't you get my messages? I left you at least two voicemails, if not three. Did you change phones?"

He stopped his movement, then turned to face her. "No. I didn't change my phone, and I did get your messages. I'm sorry I didn't call you back."

She waited for a further explanation but didn't get one. "Well, okay. But I thought it was odd that when I invited you to Stella's rescue celebration party at the Inn, you said you and Emma had something you couldn't easily change, but when I saw Emma that very night, she knew nothing of the party."

His eyebrows slowly raised and his lips pursed.

"What gives, Jeremy?"

His blinking increased in pace. "I'm sorr-…"

"Stop apologizing and explain."

He went motionless, his eyes locked on hers. His tongue slid over his lips, as if his mouth had suddenly gone dry. "Okay, let's sit."

They found the chairs to the kitchen table and sat facing each other. He ran a hand through his hair, leaving strands of it ruffled. "I'm out of my element here, Marianne. I don't want to cause trouble. But the last thing I want to do is lie to you."

She shook her head. "Why would you need to lie to me?" A chill slipped down her spine and she shivered.

"I didn't want to cause any problems at the party, so I …"

"Problems? You found her, Jeremy! You rescued her. If it weren't for you, she would've spent more hours out there. You're our hero! How could that be a problem?"

"You're sweet, and I love you." He reached out and grabbed her arm. "But there's also the camp that thinks that

Stella's abduction was my fault. Well, my indirect fault, anyway."

"What, because of your relationship with Emma?"

He gave a sideways nod. "That, and back to why Mr. Slotky was so mad at me to begin with. The bankruptcy, the layoffs, you know."

"Life happens, Jeremy. You didn't do anything deliberately to put Stella in danger."

"No. But all this is a consequence of my past mistakes."

"Which you've served your sentence for."

"Which I still have a lot of making up to do … for."

"Which you're doing, every day."

He sighed, dropped his head. "I'm trying."

She stood, then sat again. "Wait a minute. You said there's a camp that thinks Stella's abduction was your fault. Has someone actually told you that?"

He stood and took a few steps away. "I don't want to …"

She followed him. "Someone did. Who was it? That's terrible, Jeremy. Who was it?"

He turned swiftly toward her. "No. I'm not going to do this."

She studied him. "One of the search and rescue volunteers?"

"No." Jeremy picked up a clean cloth lying on one of his pieces and swiped it on the top of a chest.

"Wait. Someone told you it was your fault. And you said you didn't want to cause trouble. Was it Tom? Did Tom tell you that Stella's abduction was your fault? Because if he did, he didn't mean it, Jeremy. It was probably in the emotion of the moment before you found her."

Jeremy shook his head. "I don't want to talk about it, Marianne. Seriously. Subject closed."

Marianne squinted as she stared at her brother. Although he'd always been a little uncomfortable about her favors — the place to stay, the meals, the help with marketing his business — he never avoided her. And he loved being with his family. Too much time had been lost. He would never have missed that party without a little convincing.

"Did Tom tell you not to come to Stella's party?"

Jeremy dropped the cloth and stubbornly kept his gaze on the chest.

"That's it, isn't it? Tom told you you weren't welcome. And that's why you didn't come, and that's why you didn't even tell Emma about it." Her head was swimming and she headed for the door. Jeremy caught her arm as she breezed by.

"Sis, please, drop it. He's doing what he thinks is right. I'm not going to stand in the way of a man taking care of his family. I'd rather back out than cause problems."

She wringed her arm from his grasp and stuck an index finger in his nose. "No. We're going to talk about this, he and I. This is just plain wrong."

She stormed out the door. The items she needed at the store were the furthest thing from her mind now as she drove home. When she entered the Inn and saw Tom standing behind the guest desk, alone, her single-minded goal took highest priority.

She grabbed his arm and started pulling him to their private quarters.

"Hey, babe, whoa, whoa." His voice contained amusement and a little laughter. Well, not for long.

"We need to talk." She opened their apartment door and attempted to push him inside. Of course, his bulk didn't allow her to push him around — physically — without his acquiescence. A sturdy six foot two, two hundred twenty pounds on a good day, no one was moving him if he didn't want to go. But the anger that had simmered in her during the short drive across the island formed a tiny shot of adrenaline, which was known to do wonders for strength.

"You told Jeremy not to come to Stella's party. And you never told me." Might as well get right to the point.

He didn't flinch. Which told her that he wasn't sorry. "You better believe I did. Stella's abduction never would've happened if it weren't for Jeremy."

She gave her head an angry shake. "You mean if it weren't for Gary Slotky. This wasn't Jeremy's fault."

"Jeremy's actions produced a domino effect, culminating in Stella's abduction by his girlfriend's father. Sure, Jeremy didn't kidnap her himself. He didn't intend for this to happen. But that doesn't eliminate his guilt either."

Marianne couldn't help it. Her rage escaped her with a shriek of annoyance targeted at the man in front of her. "That's ridiculous. Jeremy found her! Jeremy saved her and brought her home, safe and sound."

Tom shook his head. "But he wouldn't have needed to if he hadn't caused the problem to begin with."

"You're talking about ancient history, Tom. Jeremy made mistakes that had horrible consequences. But he was indicted and he went to jail. He gave a decade of his life, serving his sentence. Now, he's got his life back. You're trying him again. That's not fair. And I won't put up with it."

Tom shut his mouth tight, his lips pursing, like he was trying to keep words in. He stared at her for several moments, then turned his back. He walked slowly to the couch and dropped himself into it. "Sweetheart, I love you, I always have. One of the things I love most about you is your fierce loyalty to family. But I gotta tell you, honey, I think you've got your priorities backward right now."

Marianne took a few swift steps and landed in front of him. "What are you talking about?" she asked, the fierceness in her voice surprising even herself.

"Now, now. Take a breath. Calm down. Listen to me. I know you're almost always right, and you're used to assuming that you're right. But you gotta open your mind to the possibility that you aren't quite there on this one."

"What, you think you're right and I'm wrong? In supporting my brother? I don't think so."

"See, there you go. You got your shackles up and not listening to reason."

"Because what you're suggesting is wrong. Jeremy has worked hard and he deserves our support. And if he's not going to get yours, then for darn sure, he's going to get mine."

Tom sighed and looked up at her. "You need to put your own family first, before your extended family."

"Meaning?"

"Your priorities should be me and Stella. Not Jeremy."

A line of rage rose through her esophagus and Marianne strode to the far side of the room. "I've always made you and Stella my priorities. I'm insulted that you'd suggest otherwise. But that doesn't mean that I can't make Jeremy a priority too. And my dad. And Leslie. There's room in here," she pounded her chest with a fist, "for everyone, Tom. That's just who I am. I'm shocked that you don't know that about me."

"You've got a big heart," he said quietly.

"You had no right to tell Jeremy not to come to the party — *his* party, in a way. And you deceived me by not telling me.

You let me think he didn't come because he didn't want to come."

Tom nodded. "Okay, I could've handled that better. But I didn't tell you because I knew you didn't agree with me. And I know we'll never see eye to eye on this topic."

Marianne scoffed. "Good to know that when we have disagreements, you do whatever you want and then lie to me about it."

"I did it to protect Stella. I won't apologize for that."

"There's no need to protect Stella from Jeremy!"

"And I think there is." He rose wearily to his feet and approached her. "I don't want Jeremy around Stella, Marianne. For her own safety."

Marianne shrugged angrily. "And I want Stella to have a relationship with her Uncle Jeremy. So, where does that leave us?"

Tom dropped his head. "I'm not changing my mind on this."

"Neither am I."

The urge to stomp out of the room and slam the door was tempting. But a moment of satisfaction would lead to hours of regret for handling this situation childishly. Despite herself, she faced him. "So, what do we do?" They so rarely fought. They were almost always on the same page, or at least close enough to compromise. She could never remember an issue in their entire relationship when they were on such opposite ground.

He took a deep breath and let it out. "Let's try to get some distance from this. Feel like that dressy night out?"

"No." The word popped out of her mouth before she even thought about it. But instincts usually served her well. The last thing she wanted to do was get dressed up, go out with Tom and either talk more about this, or avoid talking about this. "Not tonight."

He reached out and brushed a hand over her elbow. She kept herself from flinching at his touch. "Come on, baby. I think we need a night out. Together."

At that moment, she detested him. Sure, he was the love of her life, the one she'd devoted her present and future to, the one she'd shared her dreams with. But right now, he was the enemy. This issue was important. This disagreement held weight. It couldn't just be swept away with a pricey dinner and high heels.

He didn't understand how important this was to her, or he wouldn't be suggesting that they sweep it under the rug with a fun evening out. That was the furthest possibility from her mind. But she couldn't put her thoughts into words for him to understand. So, retreat was the best solution.

"I actually think we need some time apart. I'm going to take Stella over to my dad's. You stay here."

He studied her for a moment. "I don't feel comfortable about you badmouthing me to your dad and Leslie."

Her eyes widened. "Then maybe you ought to rethink this ultimatum you're handing me."

"I never gave you an ultimatum."

"Oh yes, you did. You told my brother he wasn't welcome in my house, without my knowledge. That's an ultimatum in my book. Him or you." At long last, the sting of tears hit her eyes and she sniffed. "Honestly, Tom, my choice is not clear to me."

She knew by his reaction that her words had stung him. She hadn't really intended to cause him pain, but wasn't sorry that she had. If he thought she would willingly disown her brother just because Tom asked her to, well, he had no idea who she was. And what kind of marriage was that?

Chapter Nine

Marianne pulled her car into the sanded driveway in front of The Old Gray Barn, the big beach house on stilts where her dad and his new bride lived. Stella unbuckled her seatbelt and jumped out of her booster seat, then disappeared out of the passenger side door. Marianne headed toward the stairs that led to the wooden front porch and realized her daughter wasn't following her. She looked back and smiled. Stella was on her knees in the sand beside the car, letting it sift through her fingers.

Marianne headed over. "Have you found anything worth saving?"

"Yes!" Stella held up a tiny conch shell, perfectly formed, but miniature. Like, less than a centimeter. The entire driveway was filled with them, mixed in with the sand. Leslie had told Stella that when she was a little girl and had come right here to this very house on vacation, she'd spend an hour with a colander from the kitchen, sifting and sifting the sand through, ending with a treasure trove of baby conch shells, which she'd present to her Barbie doll collection as gifts. Stella was so enchanted by her description, she did the same thing each time she came here.

"Perfect. Come show Grandma Leslie. She'll love it."

They walked up the wooden stairs to the porch, across the deck and after a quick knock, inside. The house was as plain and utilitarian as it was magical. Rugged wooden slats made up the floor of the entire level — the great room, an eating room, the kitchen and three bedrooms. Upstairs were two dormitory style rooms capable of holding an army of kids on vacation. And in the house's past life as a vacation rental, Marianne was sure it had, on many occasions. But now, it belonged to her dad and Leslie, who treasured it as their dream home.

Stella spotted Leslie first. She ran, holding up the mini-conch between her forefinger and thumb. "Grandma Leslie, look!"

Leslie grinned. "Good girl! Do you have a Barbie who might like that?"

"Yeah." In her excitement, her southern accent converted the word to two syllables: yay-uh. "But I need more."

"I thought you'd say that, so look what I got ready for you." She gestured to the big table. On it sat a colander from the kitchen.

Stella squealed as she grabbed it and headed for the front door.

"You want to sift by yourself, or wait for me to sift with you when your mama leaves?"

"Both!" the little girl shouted right before the door slammed after her.

Leslie beamed. The woman loved kids, and the feeling was mutual. All those years of teaching showed.

"I'm not leaving," Marianne said flatly.

"You're not? Tom called …"

"Yes, I know. Plans have changed."

Leslie studied her for a moment, then said, "Oh my. Let's get us some drinks and go out to the back porch."

Marianne nodded and followed Leslie to the kitchen, leaning against the doorframe. Leslie reached into the refrigerator and pulled out a jug of iced tea and a bottle of wine, lifting both of them, a question. Marianne took a deep breath and pointed to the wine.

A minute later, they sat on the back porch, a spacious screened in structure that faced the ocean. It reminded Marianne of the Seaside Inn's back porch, but it was smaller, more intimate. The beach was smaller too. But still gorgeous. The sound of the calm waves moving slowly in and out was balm to her itchy soul.

"Where's Dad?"

"Taking a shower."

"Oh." Funny how she'd only known Leslie about nine months, but when she needed a woman's ear, a shoulder to cry on or common-sense advice, this was the first person she thought to seek out.

"So, what's up? Why aren't you and Tom going out to dinner after all? You're not worried about leaving Stella here, are you?"

"No, no, not at all. It would've been good for Stella to spend the evening with you. You could spoil her, get your Stella fix." Marianne sighed. "But Tom and I are fighting and I couldn't stomach spending what was supposed to be a romantic night with him, pretending that I'm not absolutely furious with him." Her pulse raced through her veins with the anger of her words.

Leslie put a hand on her shoulder and let it lie there. They both stayed silent and let the waves absorb them. "Married couples fight, sweetie. It's part of the deal. Men are from Mars, you know."

Marianne smiled. "I know. But Tom and I don't fight all that often. And never about something this important. I've never known him to be so wrong before. Like, way off."

Leslie turned in her rocking chair to face her. "This sounds big. You can tell me what it is, or you don't have to. But ponder on this a moment. Is there any way you can see his point of view? Any way to give him the benefit of the doubt and try to understand it from his vantage point?"

Marianne thought while tears escaped her eyes. Soon she was wiping the moisture off her cheeks. "Not without disowning one member of my family."

Leslie's eyes popped wider. "Oh my."

Hank wandered onto the porch. "Ah," he said, "two of my most beautiful ladies. Where's my third?"

Marianne turned away and subtly wiped her eyes while Leslie said, "Stella's out in the driveway, sifting sand."

Hank laughed. "One of her favorite pastimes. That, and digging in the sand out back. Doesn't take much to please that little girl."

Her face mended enough, Marianne stood and gave her dad a hug. "Hey, Daddy." But she couldn't fool him. He held on to her tight, rubbing her back, then pulled away to study her face.

"What's going on, sweetheart?"

Her voice threatened to falter so she took a moment. Leslie replied, "She and Tom are having a disagreement."

"Ah, baby doll," he said. "Fights are okay. As long as you can come out the other side still in love." He stood uncertainly, probably wondering if he should make his escape.

"Tom wants to keep Jeremy away from Stella. He thinks Jeremy is a danger to her," she blurted. She had a mild pleasure seeing her dad and stepmom's shocked reaction to her outrageous statement. Of course they would agree with her. And the more people she could round up to disagree with Tom, the more ammunition she'd have against him to change his mind.

Marianne plopped into a rocking chair. The others were motionless.

"Why does he think that?" Hank asked.

"He thinks it's Jeremy's fault that Stella was kidnapped. That if Jeremy hadn't been in Stella's life, she wouldn't have been taken."

Hank walked slowly over to a chair beside her and sat, too. "Hmm, let's take a look at this. Jeremy didn't cause Stella's abduction."

"I know! Of course he didn't. Tom's being ridiculous."

"But Slotky only did what he did to get back at Jeremy. So from that perspective, I can see where Tom's going with this."

"Daddy! How can you say that? You know how hard Jeremy worked in prison and since he's been released, to overcome his past mistakes. This isn't fair!"

"It's not fair, darlin', but the Lord never promised us fair. It's part of life. Jeremy knows that. He deals with that every single day."

She sputtered in her outrage to his words. "He deals with it from the idiots that meet him on the street and don't know what a great man he is, a man of God who is following his faith. Not from his very own family! We should all be supporting him."

"And we are."

"Yes, *we* are. The three of us. But my husband has now decided that Jeremy is no longer welcome in our home. And when he made that decision, I seriously have to reconsider how a man I supposedly love, can come up with that."

"Now, sweetheart, don't jump the gun. Time heals all wounds. Give it some time and either Tom will come around, or you will. Tom's a good man. He's trying to protect his daughter after a terrible event. You can't blame him for that."

"Oh, yes I can! Of course he can protect Stella. But not at the cost of shutting my brother out. That's not only disrespectful to Jeremy, it's disrespectful to me. And you."

Hank reached over and grasped her hand. "Fear does a strange thing to a man. He's terrified that something bad will happen to Stella on his watch. So now he's battening down the hatches around those he loves. No way will anything like this happen again, not as long as he's around. Remember, sweetheart, he doesn't really know Jeremy. You met him and married him while Jeremy was away. He doesn't have any allegiance to Jeremy."

Marianne shook her head, the fight exhausting her. "But I do. And so, he should. It's as simple as that."

Hank stood. "You're a grown woman and will make your own decisions. This is a tough one. I know how fiercely you love your brother. But just remember, Tom's your husband. You and he are partners in life, in raising Stella. You're not always going to agree, but you do need to get past this somehow."

"I agree. Not by shutting Jeremy out of our lives, however."

Hank nodded. "Maybe you can settle on a compromise." He took a few steps toward the door. "I'll leave you wise ladies to figure this out."

Leslie murmured, "Chicken," then chuckled. "Care for a walk on the beach?"

Marianne looked over at her. "Okay."

* * *

She spent the evening at The Old Gray Barn and headed back only when Stella could barely keep her eyes open. She carried her into the Seaside Inn, and back into their apartment. Tom sat in the living room, watching television. His head jerked up when she entered. He was about to speak and Marianne gave him a "shhh" and pointed at the slumbering girl in her arms. He nodded and turned back to the tv.

Marianne carried her into the bedroom, laid her down and pulled off her clothes as best she could without waking her. Once she was down to her shirt and underwear, she pulled the blanket over her, leaned and positioned a kiss on Stella's forehead. "I love you," she whispered, and remained, her cheek brushing her daughter's. She could lay here in this dark sweetness all night, her daughter's sleepy scent encircling her senses.

Reluctantly she got up and left, closing the door behind her. Their tiny apartment within the Inn didn't leave her many options if she wanted to avoid her husband, so she returned to the living room.

"She have fun at her Paw Paw's house?"

Marianne nodded and sat, not on the couch beside him but in the easy chair close by. His gaze followed her, her selection not lost on him. "Tom, it's going to take me a while to come to terms with this decision you made."

He scooted to the end of the couch to be closer to her. "Marianne, I'm sorry for going behind your back about Stella's party. That was wrong of me. I should've included you in that from the very beginning and not tried to hide it from you."

Well, it was a start. But not nearly enough. "The fact that you hid it from me was wrong, and I accept your apology. But the bigger issue is about making Jeremy not welcome in our home. I'm never going to agree with you on that. You need to think about what you're asking me to do, and you need to come to terms with having Jeremy around here. He's part of the family."

Tom blinked. "Part of my job as Stella's father is to protect her."

"Agreed. She's no longer in any danger. The bad guy's been arrested. He's in jail."

"For now."

"Yes, for now. And we'll stay on top of his trial. If for some unforeseeable reason he's acquitted, we'll take steps then. But Slotky is the bad guy here, *not* Jeremy."

"I realize that. But Jeremy carries with him a decade of associations that I don't want anywhere near Stella. Slotky was one. Who's next? She's my little precious angel. I don't want her exposed to that element."

Marianne sighed and rose. "I refuse to discuss this with you right now. I'm exhausted and going to bed. And Tom …" she looked around the room "…I'm not up to sleeping together tonight. I'm too hurt, I'm too angry, I'm too emotional."

"What are you suggesting?" he said with a frown.

"I'll bring you a sheet and a blanket. You can sleep on the couch."

He looked like he would reply but she didn't give him the chance. She went to fetch the bedding, plopped the stack on the couch, and escaped to their bedroom.

Chapter Ten

The Millers from Wisconsin were checking out. Marianne prepared their final bill and they handed over a credit card.

"It was such a pleasure to have you back this year."

Mrs. Miller smiled. "We had a wonderful time. The Inn is so quaint, the beach is wonderful. And the food …? Oh my goodness, your chef has to be the best in the area. In fact, the food is even better than I remember from the last two winters we've stayed here. Did you get a new chef?"

"Nope, same one, but I added another part-time kitchen worker so Toby can focus more on menu design and cooking the main courses, and he can delegate the side dishes."

"Perfect. Lovely. Delicious."

The transaction complete, Marianne texted Tom. "If you'll wait just a second, Tom will be here to carry your luggage to your car. I also wanted to tell you that we are now offering a discount for repeat reservers. If you reserve your spot for your next stay with just a two-week down payment, we'll take 10% off your entire stay."

"That's a good deal!" Mrs. Miller looked excitedly at her husband. He glanced at her as he tucked his card back in his wallet, then gave a curt shake of his head.

Mrs. Miller sighed and turned back to Marianne. "We're not ready to reserve today. How long is the offer good for?"

The offer, as designed, was only good until they stepped foot out of the Inn. Of course, she and Tom were the designers of the deal so she had the authority to extend it. "How long do you need to finalize your plans?"

Mr. Miller wandered over to his stack of luggage and Mrs. Miller lowered her voice. "I'm not sure. I'm dying to come back. But I have to convince him. He wants to go somewhere else."

"Would it be rude to inquire why? Was it something we could've done better?"

"I'm not sure what his problem is. We've had three lovely winters here. Suddenly in the last few days he's started talking about going somewhere else."

"The last few days?"

"Yes. He knows I'm set on coming back. I'm not sure why the discount didn't do it for him."

Marianne studied the older woman and went ahead and asked what was on her mind. "Do you think it could be because of the issues we've had this winter? The fire in the storage shed, and the scare with Stella being taken?"

Mrs. Miller stared, her eyes going wide. "You know, that could be it, now that you mention it. He's not one to talk much. But I know the fire really shook him. He's asthmatic so he has trouble breathing in other than ideal environments. And when the news came out that the kidnapper of your adorable little girl was actually posing here at the Inn as a snowbird, I bet it got him thinking. Why put yourself at danger? There are so many other places to choose from."

Marianne nodded. "I'm so sorry."

Mrs. Miller gripped her forearm. "No, honey, none of this is your fault. But definitely could have an impact on my husband. I hope you don't have a significant decrease in business because of this."

She gave a small wave and joined Tom and her husband with the bags. "Thank you, Mrs. Miller. And if you want a little time to think about reserving, that discount will be good for another week."

Tom gave her a look on his way to the door, but she didn't care.

She was 90% sure the Millers wouldn't return, as a direct result of the trouble with Slotky. She was 75% sure that the other departing guests who declined reserving for next year, did so because of the same reason. She had to do something, or her whole business and way of life would be over.

Her fingers shaking, she pulled up a search engine on her computer. She spent the next forty minutes searching for ideas of additional ways to attract guests to the Inn. When Tom came in and wanted to talk about the extension on the discount offer, she waved him off. When she was done, she had a list of ideas she'd consider pursuing.

She wasn't about to go down without swinging.

* * *

Tom stopped his work of straightening the contents of the storage shed and put his hands on both hips, stretching his back slowly. The cricks and creaks expelled from his spine made him grimace. That couch was not the place to sleep for his demanding lumbar. The high-priced mattress in their bedroom, perfect for spinal alignment, was where he should be. Maybe after a night on the couch, Marianne would welcome him back.

His mind meandered to ideas to help sweeten the deal — candy, flowers. Those were usually surefire ways to put a smile on her face. Any thoughtful gift to make her realize how often she's on his mind. Because she was, constantly, on his mind. After seven years of marriage, a child and the pressures of working together every day, she was still the woman of his dreams. The woman he loved and wanted to spend the rest of his life with.

But small, meaningless gifts like flowers and candy didn't strike him as the most effective offerings now. He and his wife were too far apart on the ends of the spectrum. One of them would have to give in. He was feeling way too strongly about this topic for it to be him.

A childhood memory came to mind. Tom's brother, Rod was the family hellion. Until Rod came along, the family was pretty normal and stable. Tom and his sister Lori were model kids. Sure, they got in trouble like any other kids, but never for anything crazy. And their punishments were more verbal than physical. His parents had it made. They rarely raised their voices. That's how he and Marianne were bringing Stella up. Deal with her maturely, with reason. Get her to understand the right way, then reward her for following it.

Life was good until their little brother Rod was about ten. For such a young kid, he sure knew how to raise hell. From the time he bounced a basketball in the center of Mom's extravagantly set Thanksgiving dinner table, to the time he punched a teacher in the face and got kicked out of public school, Rod never seemed to be happy unless he was causing trouble.

Tom had observed the toll these events took on his parents. His mother, so sweet and kind, had to learn how to be tough to handle this type of kid. His father developed a loud, firm voice Tom had never heard before. Family outings reduced in frequency and most of family time was figuring out how to respond to Rod's latest escapade.

The years passed. Rod usually only stayed at each school for a year, then on to the next. His teen years arrived and the violations grew worse. Now, his mishaps drew the police. Burglaries, truancy, minor acts of violence. His mother withdrew into herself, at a loss as to how to raise this deviant child.

One night, Mom sat in her nightgown in their living room, her feet curled beneath her, watching television. A peaceful evening after a hard day's work was interrupted by the sound of glass splintering, followed by a brick landing clumsily in the middle of the room. Mom screamed and jumped to her feet. Dad yelled, "What was that?" from another room. Tom ran down the hallway from his bedroom, just in time to see and hear a hot rod squealing away on the street outside of their calm, normal all-American neighborhood.

Seventeen-year-old Tom saw a change in his dad after that. The lines in his face hardened as he stood, arms around his terrified family. Danger and evil had invaded his home, his family. And he wasn't going to stand idly by and let that happen.

Things moved fast after that. Mom and Dad evicted Rod from their home. He wasn't welcome there anymore. While his parents were busy filing papers to make Rod a ward of the state, basically disowning him and disavowing themselves as responsible for his actions, Rod stole a car and started driving west. He made it all the way to California before he was arrested and sent to juvie.

By the time he'd been locked up a year, the paperwork came through. Rod Mueller was no longer recognized a dependent child of James and Ellen Mueller. He was a ward of the state, incarcerated indefinitely in juvenile detention in California. Other than an occasional short back and forth between his mom and his brother, their connection was cut off. His parents were no longer responsible for paying the damages his brother inflicted. At least, his monetary damages. They would all be held to paying the emotional damages caused by his brother, for a long time to come.

In the shed, Tom shook his head, clearing it of ancient family history. He pulled his cell phone out of his pocket and called his dad.

"Hey, Pops."

"Tom! How's it going?"

"Fine, just fine. I was thinking of you and thought I'd give you a call."

"Glad you did. How's that sweet little granddaughter of mine?"

Tom found a bench in the dark shed and sat. "Amazingly well, Dad. Seems like we dodged a bullet. She's the same happy little girl she's always been."

"That's great, Tommy. Glad to hear it."

"Although, Marianne and I are taking her to counseling, just to be sure. Gives her someone unbiased to talk to about the kidnapping, and the counselor reports to us if there's any problems we need to be aware of. But so far, everything's great."

"Terrific."

"How are you and Mom?"

"Doing good, son. You and Marianne?"

"Good."

"Great."

Tom stifled a chuckle. So went every conversation he and his dad had ever had. Very little talking, topics just on the surface. "Well, I'm cleaning out the shed behind the Inn."

"Okay, you sound busy. Thanks for calling, son."

"Maybe we can get you and Mom out here for Memorial Day. Have a cookout on the beach."

"Oh, that sounds great. We'll plan it."

"Love you, Pops."

"Love you too."

Tom pocketed the phone and went back to work.

* * *

At dinner time, Marianne sat with Stella in the dining room. Tom entered and she lifted a hand and waved him over. Because the Inn was depleting of snowbirds and the spring breakers hadn't yet arrived, only four tables besides theirs was occupied.

Stella lifted her arms up for her upside down hug from her daddy and Tom leaned over and embraced her.

"What's for dinner?" he asked as he sat across from her.

"Fried chicken," she said, distracted by the topic she needed to discuss with him. "But before we eat, Tom, I want to show you this. I've done some research I want to share with you." She straightened her research papers, folded her hands over them and met eyes with him. "You know I've been worried about our declining rate of return visitors. More and more snowbirds who are checking out are unwilling to commit to reserving their spot next year. I've been offering the 10% discount the last few weeks and haven't had a single taker. At this rate, the entire Inn will be empty next winter."

Tom nodded cautiously. If she could get him to understand the gravity of the situation, hopefully she could get him to support her solution.

"You know as well as I do that at any given time, we can operate with some empty rooms. To make ends meet we need to be at half capacity at all times. Three quarter capacity is a good target for the fall and winter months, and full capacity for the spring and summer. I'm really concerned that we're not going to hit those goals this year.

"So, I've done some research. I've looked at ideas that other Inns our size have done and I've come up with something I want to try. I think we have the space and the means, and best of all, I think it'll be a fun project. And … it could draw a lot of traffic."

She smiled and pulled out her top piece of paper … a sample flyer she'd created this afternoon.

He stared, lines creasing his forehead. "Music Man? You want to offer music lessons here?"

His obtuseness irritated her but she was determined not to let him rain on her enthusiasm for her idea. "No. Dinner theater!" She stood up and made a slow circle, gesturing throughout the dining room. "Right here! We have a huge space here that's rarely utilized to its fullest. We put a stage on this wall, add more tables, a cash bar. We could seat one hundred in here for dinner and a show, every weekend. We'd draw not only our resident guests, but theater lovers from the island, from Myrtle and nearby communities."

Tom's cheeks puffed out, then released a loud puff of air. He shut his mouth, then ventured, "Really?"

"Yes. Now listen, I've done my homework on this, Tom. Dinner theaters are very popular. We'll serve our normal dinner selections, just to a much larger crowd. By adding on the show, we could charge thirty-five or forty dollars per person. Once the show is produced, we could run it as long as there is interest, every weekend. It'll get people in the door that we'd never attract as overnight guests.

"Now, the show selection. I found out musicals are more popular than non-musicals, and *The Music Man* is one of the most popular musicals in history. Everyone is familiar with the show and the music. Another reason I picked it is there's a large cast of children. Who wouldn't want to come see their kid perform in a play? I think it'll draw a big crowd."

Tom ran a quick hand over his mouth, his whisker stubble scraping. "Marianne, hold on here. I understand you're trying to find ways to get more people in the door. That's great. But … not this. You know what this sounds like to me? Expensive."

Marianne shrugged. "Not particularly…"

"Oh come on, babe. A stage? Sets, scripts, costumes, instruments, musicians, directors, actors, lighting. Oh my gosh. All that costs money. I don't think you've thought this through. How could we possibly break even on this, let alone make money on it?"

"We could ask for donors. Businesses to sponsor us and in return, we'll advertise them in our program. You never know until you ask. In fact, there's a community theater in Myrtle Beach. Maybe we could borrow a bunch of that stuff from them."

Tom sat back in his seat, crossed his arms over his chest. "No. I'm sorry, sweetheart, this is too risky. Too expensive, too big an undertaking and we're not equipped for it. And there's absolutely no guarantee of a profit. Most likely, we'd spend more than we'd ever recoup. I can't approve this, I'm sorry. Find something else."

His verdict relayed, he leaned forward, picked up his napkin and draped it over his lap. He turned his head toward the kitchen, probably looking for his fried chicken. She was dismissed, totally and completely. The hours she'd spent researching, Googling and brainstorming, done. Over. With one rejection from Tom.

Well, Tom wasn't the final word. She was a co-owner of this Inn. They ran it together. Her decision was just as important as his. He couldn't veto her idea unless she backed down and let him.

And today, that was the last thing she wanted to do.

Sure, putting on a full-scale musical theater production was going to be challenging. She had no real experience doing anything like this before. But she was resourceful, and had a lot of friends, and she felt sure she could bring in the expertise she needed to pull it off. And the expense — poo, you had to spend money to make money. Her research showed that theater productions were very popular, with vacationers and residents alike. They'd never offered one before. What harm could it possibly be to try it? If it didn't work out, at least they'd given it a shot. They'd tried something new. But she refused to a) sit back and let her Inn decline without doing something about it and b) give up on *The Music Man* just because Tom had listened to her idea for less than five minutes and said no.

She looked up at him. "I don't accept your veto."

The server slid a plate of fried chicken, fried potatoes and collard greens into place in front of him, then did the same for Leslie and Stella. Marianne smiled at her until the girl moved on.

Tom picked up a fork. "What do you mean?"

Marianne shrugged. "I want to pursue *The Music Man* idea. You want to veto it. I don't accept your veto. Simple as that."

He took a sample of collard greens, then put his fork down. "So let me get this straight. Despite the fact that I don't support you spending all the time, money and effort to produce a dinner theater, you're going to do it anyway?"

She always knew he had it in him. "That's right."

"Marianne, we own this Inn together. We've always made business decisions together."

"This is the first revolutionary, creative idea one of us has ever had. And the other one of us wants to quash it. I'm not going to let you."

Tom set his fork down. "I don't mean to quash your creativity. I just think it's going to be a lot of work and a lot of money, with very little chance at being profitable."

She nodded. "You've made your concerns clear. But I've done the research and I think you're wrong. I'm moving ahead with the idea."

His mouth dropped open and his eyes scanned her face.

"Don't worry, it'll be my project. I'll do all the work and bring people in to help as needed. I'll keep you informed of my progress, but I won't ask you for any help. While I'm focused on the dinner theater, I'd appreciate it if you handled the day-to-day operations of the Inn."

Tom pushed his plate of steaming dinner a couple inches away. "Marianne, this is crazy. I don't like where this is going."

"Where what is going?"

He sighed, then pushed his chair back and stood. "This decision, our business, our marriage." He looked around as if suddenly aware he was standing and speaking with a raised voice in the middle of a room full of paying guests. He sat.

"We need to talk about this and come to a decision we both feel good about."

"That doesn't seem to be possible lately. Every decision we face, you're on one side, I'm on the other. We don't see eye to eye, and we don't have any agreement. But you're dealing with ultimatums and absolutes. You don't want Jeremy to be around Stella, and you just expect me to accept that. You don't like my idea for a dinner theater, so you want to put your fist down and I just don't do it. Well, it's not going to work that way, Tom. I disagree with you, on both counts. And you can't just issue an order and expect me to obey it. That's not a marriage."

Tom lifted his hands and rubbed his eyes. "Sweetheart, I don't mean to come across like that. But I am the head of the household. I have certain decisions to make, and although they're not popular, I have good reasons for making them. Do I want to force these decisions down your throat? No. You're my wife. An equal partner. I want to have a calm conversation about these things so you understand where I'm coming from. But you've got the bristles up on your back and refuse to listen to reason."

Suddenly, a wave of exhaustion came over her. The wind went out of her sails. Did he have a valid point? Was she so determined to be right, that she wasn't being reasonable? She needed time to think. Time to pray, time to ponder.

"Tom, do me a favor tonight. After dinner will you take Stella? Do her bedtime routine with her — bath, story, pajamas. I'm going to check into one of the empty guest rooms tonight."

"You're leaving me?"

The pain and desperation in his voice had her head coming up fast to meet his eyes. "Not exactly. I mean, it's no secret we're having problems. We need to solve them. In order for me to see my actions and motivations more clearly, I need some space, some quiet. I need some uninterrupted time. You understand?"

He nodded reluctantly. "All night?"

"Yes."

He took a deep breath and let it out. "Take the time you need. I want to work this out, Marianne."

"So do I. I just don't want to lose myself in the midst of it."

* * *

An hour later, Marianne sat in one of their cozy guest rooms, the light bleached wood floors covered with a hand-braided throw rug, the window thrown open to the scent and sound of the ocean waves. Settled into the rocking chair, she started with a silent prayer.

Dear God, please watch over Tom and me. Please help us communicate and see eye to eye. Let us remember to love each other. And God, prepare my heart for learning. If I'm wrong, please help me to see it. I mean, knock me over the head with it. Make it unmistakable. Thank you. Amen.

She kept her eyes closed for a moment, then opened them. She really meant it. Introspection was not a strength of hers. She sure *felt* right in her convictions. But in order to prevent going down a path in her marriage that she couldn't return from, she wanted to know if she was being stubborn and unreasonable. Even if it was hard to hear.

She opened the laptop she'd brought from the apartment and Googled for a Bible website. Then she searched until she found what she was looking for: the role of the husband and wife in a marriage.

She read, "First Peter, chapter 3. Wives, in the same way submit yourselves to your husbands so that, if any of them do not believe the word, they may be won over without words by the behavior of their wives, when they see the purity and reverence of your lives."

She sat back and let her mind wander over the verses. It appeared to be referring to wives being responsible for living in a godly and Christian-like way in order to win their husbands over to belief in God, in case he didn't believe to begin with. That didn't really apply to her and Tom. One thing she'd always loved about him was his faith in God, and his determinedness to live a life following the Lord.

She looked back at the laptop. "Husbands, in the same way be considerate as you live with your wives, and treat them with respect as the weaker partner and as heirs with you of the gracious gift of life, so that nothing will hinder your prayers."

See, this was the kind of Bible verse that didn't seem to apply to the modern generation. A weaker partner? She didn't consider herself a weaker partner in her marriage. Tom had his role, and she had hers, both in their business together, and their parenting of Stella. But they were equal partners in life. She liked the part that said, "heirs with you of the gracious gift of life." That had a nice ring to it. But her ... a weaker partner? No way.

But did Tom think of her that way? He had said he was the head of the household, and he had made a decision, and it was her job to accept it. That sounded remarkably old-fashioned. She was a modern woman. How can you be an educated, successful, married woman in the modern age, and still follow the spirit of what the Bible says about marriage?

She searched the Bible site for "head of the household" and came up with Colossians 3: "Wives, submit to your husbands, as is fitting to the Lord. Husbands, love your wives and do not be harsh with them." So, wives had to submit to, or obey their husbands in everything, and all husbands had to do was to be nice to their wives? That certainly didn't seem like God's will.

And another reference: Ephesians 5: "Wives, submit to your husbands as to the Lord. For the husband is the head of the wife, as Christ is the head of the church. Now, as the church submits to the Lord, so wives submit to their husbands in everything."

Marianne slammed the laptop lid closed. She needed help. She needed a Bible study or a scholar to explain this concept to her. She'd been a Christian her entire life, and she never felt like God had relinquished her, as a woman, or worse, as a married woman, to just meekly go about, following her husband's commands. That was foreign to her. She had a brain, she had ambition. If that were what God wanted for females, who would willingly sign up for that kind of life?

She had to be missing something here. She opened the lid again and searched for help in interpreting these verses. She really wanted to understand God's will for her in maneuvering these bumps in the road with Tom. But she had to understand what God expected of her as a wife before she could figure out if her behavior and attitude needed adjusting.

Google provided her with an abundance of links. But it wasn't until she clicked on one about halfway down the page, that the understanding dawned like a beach sunrise.

Ephesians 5 continues, "Husbands, love your wives, just as Christ loved the church and gave himself up for her to make her holy, cleansing her by the washing with water through the word, and to present her to himself as a radiant church, without stain or wrinkle or any other blemish, but holy and blameless. In this same way, husbands ought to love their wives as their own bodies. He who loves his wife loves himself."

God's charge to husbands is to love their wives as Christ loved the church. That was a very high order: Christ gave himself for the church — he laid down his life for it. So, husbands are expected by God to lay down their lives for their wives, if necessary. A husband's love for his wife should be foremost in his mind, his highest priority. The authority the man has over the woman, in God's perfect plan, is founded on his love to her, and this love must be big enough to lead him to risk his life for her. And the wife, if she is a good wife as planned by God, is deserving of that level of love expected of the husband.

The wife, when looked at it in this context, is someone to be exalted.

Marianne closed the laptop and set it on the bed. Her mind was racing and her pulse was making her fingers tingle. She'd hit on something important here, she just needed time to process it. She prayed, *God, thank you for leading me to that section. You don't just look at a woman or a wife as some lesser partner who follows the man's orders. You see her as an exalted partner so worthy of her husband's respect and devotion, that he would give his life for her if necessary, just like your Son did for the church. Help me to understand that. And help me to apply that to my own life, my own marriage. I know you don't want me to turn my back on my brother, even though that's what my husband wants me to do. Help me, God, help me to find answers and comfort and peace, while helping me heal my marriage. Amen.*

Would Tom agree with this verse? Would he be willing to give his life for her or for Stella, if needed, to protect them? Her instinct told her he would. And what if the tables were turned? Would she be willing to give her life to protect or save Tom's life? But God didn't call on wives with the same expectation.

The evening passed and Marianne continued her study until she couldn't keep her eyes open.

Chapter Eleven

The next morning, Marianne slept late and woke peacefully until she grabbed her phone off the bedside table and remembered that they had their final counseling session with Stephanie and it was a family one. She threw off the covers and yanked herself to her feet, stomping for the door. She now had a little over a half hour to shower, dress, eat and get Stella ready before jumping in the car.

She ran down the hallway, down the stairs and across the great room to the apartment, praying that she didn't run into any guests while in her pajamas and her hair a mess. She breezed into their living quarters and saw Tom and Stella, dressed and clean, paging through one of her picture books.

"What the heck is going on?" she stormed.

Tom looked up, the expression on his face determinedly pleasant. "And good morning to you, Mommy."

Marianne ran a hand through her hair. The sarcasm in his voice was evident and he was right. No reason to start the day with an argument. She continued with a calm voice, "Why didn't you wake me up? Now I have to rush to get ready on time."

He gave her a bland smile. "When you chose to sleep somewhere else than your home, I figured you could manage getting yourself up on time. Stella and I have been up for nearly an hour now."

She considered that and conceded that again, he was right. This was her problem, not his. And yet …, "You did want me to go to the appointment with you, didn't you?"

"Of course. It's a full family session today."

She sighed and headed for the shower. She'd go wet headed and hungry if she had to, but she'd be ready. As the spray pelted her back, she prayed for guidance. If she could remember the way God intended marriage to be — with the man thinking so highly of his wife that he would literally give anything to protect her, and the woman being a close partner with the man, working to carry through the vision he set for the family, then maybe their marriage had a chance.

But did that idea hold a place in today's modern world? Or was that an ancient ideal that didn't translate to the 21st century?

It started with her, that much was clear. She needed to do her part as an exalted wife who deserved to be held in such high esteem. Then maybe she could get Tom to understand the error in his thinking. And she'd have to do a lot better than storming into their home first thing in the morning with anger and accusation on her mind.

She sighed. *Help me, Lord.*

They made it to the counselor's office with a few minutes to spare. Marianne's damp hair was in a ponytail and she'd eaten a protein bar in the car. They sat in the waiting room and after a brief pause, Stephanie welcomed them into her office.

"Full family session today," Stephanie said.

Tom and Marianne nodded.

"Let me start by asking Stella a few questions." She turned to Stella, who smiled up at her. "Stella, how are you doing?"

"Fine."

"Are you sleeping well?"

"Yeah."

"Nightmares?"

"Nope."

"Sweetheart, do you ever think about that man who put you in the car?"

Stella shrugged.

"You know he was a bad guy and the police got him and put him in jail, right?"

Stella nodded.

"He can't get close to you again."

"I know."

"You know your mommy and daddy keep you safe?"

She nodded again.

"Do you ever get scared to be at home around the guests at the Inn?"

"No."

Stephanie reached over and patted Stella's hand. "Do you have anything you want to talk to me about?"

Stella shrugged and shook her head.

"Do you want to go play with the toys in the corner?"

Stella gave her a big, beaming smile and jumped to her feet.

"I'd interpret that as a yes. Of course, I'm a paid professional. Go ahead, honey."

Marianne watched her daughter race to the corner and make herself comfortable to explore all the new toys. God had answered their prayers. Stella had come out the other side of this disaster without blemish. She was going to be fine. She reached over and squeezed Tom's hand. He startled at the contact, looked over at her and the corners of his lips upturned.

"Mom, Dad, you have a very well-adjusted five-year-old."

"Seriously?" Marianne asked breathlessly.

"Yep. I see no further reason for her to attend counseling. Keep an eye on her. If she develops nightmares or any anti-social behavior around the guests that is abnormal for her, feel free to call me to make an appointment. But you guys are obviously doing a good job of making her feel safe and secure. She seems fine."

Marianne let out a breath of relief. She put her hand back on her lap.

"So, how are you guys doing?"

Marianne dropped her head, stared at her lap and wondered if Tom was going to open up and be honest, or whether he would brush their troubles away like they didn't exist. Without looking at him, she answered, "Not good."

"Okay. You've been through a traumatic family event. I'd be surprised, honestly, if your response was anything else. Now, why don't I get someone to take Stella to play in another room, and you can tell me what you mean?"

She glanced over at Tom. His head was lowered, his jaw tight, his forehead creased. She nodded.

Stephanie pushed a button on an intercom near the door. Soon, a young woman entered the room and focused on Stella.

"Hey Stella, my name's Grace. How about you and I go check out some new toys and Stephanie will talk to your parents a little while?"

Stella glanced over at Marianne, and she nodded with a big smile. "We'll be done in just a little while, sweetheart." Stella took Grace's hand and followed her out the door.

She could feel tension emanating from her husband. She looked up at Stephanie who was looking at them both intently. "We disagree over where to place the blame for this incident, and how to move forward from it."

Stephanie nodded. "Go on."

"Tom thinks this is my brother, Jeremy's fault. As a result, and due to his need to protect our family, he wants to cut Jeremy completely out of our family. Of course, I can't do that."

"I think I understand Jeremy's connection to the kidnapper. But why would the kidnapping itself be Jeremy's fault?"

Marianne looked over at Tom, who didn't appear to feel compelled to answer. "My brother served ten years in jail for bad business decisions he made with my family's contracting firm. The kidnapper, Mr. Slotky, was one of the workers who got laid off when the company went bankrupt. He held a grudge."

Stephanie nodded slowly. "Okay. So Tom, tell us your thoughts on this matter."

Tom cleared his throat and straightened a little in his chair. "Jeremy, whether intentionally or not, put my daughter in danger. Jeremy has made decisions in his life that I don't want Stella to have any connection to. He has to pay the consequences for the error of his ways, but that doesn't mean that my daughter or my wife have to pay as well."

Marianne clenched her mouth shut.

Stephanie continued, "So you're saying that Jeremy, because of his past contacts that he made as a result of his crime and his stay in jail, is putting your family in danger."

"That's right."

"No, that's not right," Marianne said. "Jeremy has worked very hard, both during his incarceration and since he's been released, to be a model citizen. He made mistakes over ten years ago. He deserves a fair shot to live a normal life. Tom wants to completely disown him. But I love my brother and refuse to do that. Jeremy deserves my help and support."

Tom swung his gaze from her to Stephanie and shrugged. "And that's where we're at. I can't change my position and she can't change hers. We can't compromise."

"I see. Are you guys arguing frequently on this topic?"

"I would say, we used to. Now we've reached an angry impasse. There's no use arguing about it anymore and beating a dead horse. We're not going to come to an agreement."

"Would you say that Stella is aware of the tension between you?"

Tom said, "We make the effort not to raise our voices in front of her. The last thing we want is to make her feel unsafe or unloved. But certainly there have been changes in our home that she's picked up on."

"Like what?"

"Several nights, we haven't shared a bed."

Stephanie looked over at Marianne. "He slept on the couch one night, and I slept in a guest room last night."

"Did she ask either of you about that?"

Tom answered, "She asked me this morning where Mommy was. I just told her she was in one of the guest rooms."

"Did she seem upset about it?"

"Not particularly."

Stephanie nodded. "Tom, I'd like to delve a little deeper into your position on this. You want to shut Jeremy completely out of your family's lives?"

"Yes. I think it's in the best interest of my family, and particularly Stella, if we no longer have contact with him."

"I don't see that Jeremy intentionally put Stella in danger. I think what happened with Mr. Slotky was nothing that Jeremy could've prevented. You do realize, of course, that life hands us a lot of situations that we have no control over."

Tom clamped his mouth shut, then said, "We all take risks in life. But as Stella's father, and the head of the household, I want to limit the amount of risk we take. I've seen situations where the father kept allowing bad things to happen because he didn't want to make the hard decisions to stop it. As a result, the family unit was harmed."

"Can you tell us more about that?"

Tom sat quietly for a moment. "My brother was troubled. He never really fit into our family. To call him a black sheep is an understatement. He caused problem after problem for my parents, and I remember so many times, my mom's tears and my dad's yelling. His escapades and his connections with other bad people put all of us in danger, time and time again. He caused so much heartache for all of us, especially my parents. Finally, my dad got tough. He legally cut ties with my brother. He's no longer a part of my family."

Marianne stared. She'd heard the story of Tom's little brother Rod. But he didn't speak of it often, and she'd never talked to her in-laws about it. Could this long ago event in his own family be a driving force behind his decision about theirs?

"Did you support your father in this decision to legally cut ties with your brother?"

"Absolutely. In fact, he let it go on way too long. I wish he'd done it sooner. Life got so much more pleasant in the family once we didn't have to worry about my brother."

"Have you ever been in contact with your brother since?"

"No. None of us have. He lives his own life, and we live ours."

Marianne shook her head. She almost didn't recognize this man sitting beside her. Tom was a wonderful husband, a top-rate father to Stella. He was her chosen life partner. But she was seeing him in a new light. Maybe he was only a fair-weather partner. When things were going well, he'd work hard and love her. But now that she'd introduced a little bit of adversity into their lives, in the form of her ex-con brother, he wanted to cut ties and run.

"Life is filled with twists and turns, Tom," Marianne said. "You can't plan every path, and you certainly can't cut ties and run every time something happens that you don't like."

He looked over at her, surprise on his face. "I can make decisions to keep my family safe and sound within the boundaries of our life. I can control a lot of things, not everything. But if it's within my control, and the path seems clear, I'm not afraid to make the hard decisions."

They talked another half hour, but Marianne felt that no further progress was made. When Stephanie ended the session, she said, "I'm releasing Stella from further counseling sessions. But you guys might want to consider some couples therapy. I can refer you to a few colleagues of mine that I recommend."

Marianne nodded. "Thank you."

They checked out and left with several business cards in hand. The ride home was silent.

* * *

The rest of the day was consumed with Inn business and dinner. Back in their apartment after Stella's bedtime, Marianne had a quiet moment to talk to Tom.

"So, do you want to go to couples therapy?"

He looked over at her, muted the television and sighed. "I don't know, babe. My first impulse is to say no. We should be able to settle our own arguments and deal with our own problems. On the other hand, this is a big one; bigger than we've ever dealt with before. And we're on opposite ends of the spectrum. Maybe an unbiased opinion would help."

The thought of her life and the state of her marriage made her tired.

He reached over and took her hand. "I love you. If you want to go to counseling and try to heal our marriage, then I won't say no."

"I'm not saying I want to. I don't know, Tom. I just don't know what to do."

"I'm sorry you're not happy. But can you at least try to see my side of this thing?"

Marianne guessed she could see his point if she looked at it purely from a logical standpoint. But emotions held such a huge place in the situation. Love, loyalty, family. She couldn't tolerate his ultimatum to disown her brother. She refused to honor it.

"Tom, I want to live a godly life, a godly marriage. But this just doesn't feel right to me. What you're asking me to do is not supported by the Bible. Will you pray with me? No matter what we do, whether we go to counseling or try to solve this ourselves, we have to ask God to guide us."

He nodded. She prayed out loud, "God, we are in need of your wise counsel. We've gotten ourselves into a problem in our marriage and we can't seem to solve it alone. I want to be the kind of wife you want me to be, and a good life partner to Tom. Tom wants to protect our family and keep us all safe. But we've hit an impasse on the ways to approach this problem. We need your help. Please pour your wisdom and love over us. Please help us to love our daughter and live our lives in a way that is pleasing to you. And please make your way clear so we both understand. Amen."

* * *

The next morning, Marianne grabbed her stack of dinner theater materials and a notebook. Always a planner, she started making lists of tasks needed to make this particular dream come true. Tom walked through the great room. "Are you going to breakfast?"

She nodded. "In a minute. I'm in the middle of this and don't want to stop."

He stepped over and looked over her shoulder. "What is this?"

She looked up. "It's my To Do list for the dinner theater. I've already come up with two pages of tasks and the ideas are still coming."

He was quiet a moment. "You're pursuing that idea?"

"Yes." She jotted down, 'Talk to Leslie about directing,' then looked up at him.

"I thought we'd decided it was too expensive and too risky."

She put her pen down. "No, Tom. You decided it was too expensive and too risky. I decided to move ahead with it." She held her hand up, interrupting his protests, "I'll have regular checkpoints with you. For now, it's a lot of talking to people and deciding how we can make it work. I'm not going in blind, you know."

He frowned and hesitated. Finally, "So, you're saying you're still checking it out, and if it's clear to both of us that it is a risky investment, you won't do it?"

She smirked. "Way to put a positive spin on it, Tom. How about this? I'm still checking it out, and if I can find a way to be successful and meet our financial goals, we'll do it."

Glass half empty, meet glass full.

"Fine." And with that, he left.

The next few days were filled with busily scratching one item after another off her To Do List. By the end of a week, these decisions were in place:

The community theater in Myrtle Beach would partner with the Inn to sponsor the dinner theater. They would provide costumes and props for free and Marianne would advertise them heavily in their program.

The play was too long to perform in its entirety in the dinner theater format. Emma, who was a professional journalist and was talented in creative writing in many formats, would edit and streamline the script so it could be performed in 75 minutes.

Leslie would direct the production.

Her dad would build the stage and the sets.

Marianne would update the Inn's website with audition information and eventually, webpages to advertise their show and sell tickets. She would also design and print the programs.

Stella would play one of the town children.

Emma would use her contacts at *Seminal* Magazine and the Myrtle Beach newspaper to advertise the show once they were closer.

Marianne had a checkpoint meeting with Tom and went over the progress made, the high amount of volunteer help, and the limited expenses they'd incurred so far. She had to smile when he reluctantly agreed that they should move forward with the project.

* * *

On Saturday, Marianne sat with Stella at the table in the Inn's dining room. Her notebook containing her To Do List sat in front of her as she ate her grilled cheese sandwich. To Do Lists were awesome for several reasons: they kept her on track, and they gave her that undeniably good feeling of crossing items OFF the list. She had just crossed off "Shop for the paint for the sets." Her heart raced with pleasure. She was getting there. She was going to pull this thing off.

Then, Stella's raised voice cut into her concentration. "Mommy! Listen to me! Right now!"

Marianne's head darted up, then slowly around to see if guests were observing. Fortunately, none were. "What, sweetheart?"

"You're not listening to me, are you?"

"Of course I am. I always listen to you."

Stella looked like she was trying hard to resist an eye roll. Then she pulled out one of the tricks Marianne used with her on a semi-frequent basis, "What did I just say?"

Marianne took a sharp breath. Darn that kid using her own parenting methods against her. If she was this smart at age five, how would Marianne ever survive mothering her till she was a legal adult? Still, she took a stab. "You were saying you wanted to go outside and play in the sand." It was a valid guess. Nine times out of ten, that's exactly what Stella wanted to do.

Of course, not this time.

"No! See? You weren't listening, now admit it."

Marianne closed her notebook and physically pushed it away, out of her eyesight, out of her concentration. She folded her hands in front of her. "You're right, sweetheart. I'm busy planning the dinner theater."

"But it's Saturday!"

Yes, one of seven weekly work days here at the Inn. You didn't really get a day off when you owned your own residential business. However, she and Tom tried hard to make sure that Stella had a normal weekend filled with fun activities with her family and friends.

"You're absolutely correct. Now, how about we do something fun? What would you like to do, Miss Stella?"

"You and me?"

"Sure, you, me, whoever you want."

"Grandma Leslie?"

"Perfect. I'll call her and see if she's free. She might have plans, with this late of notice. Now, what do you have in mind?"

Stella tapped a finger on her lips. "I know! Remember Isabella's birthday party?"

Marianne frowned. "When was it, honey?"

"Last summer. We all got on the big boat and the dolphins chased us!"

Ahh, yes. A dolphin cruise. Playful dolphins jumping in and out of the wake created by a speedboat. "Great idea, honey. Let's get our sweatshirts on. It might be a little chilly."

A half hour later, Marianne and Stella jumped in the car and headed to a nearby marina. Happily, Leslie was free and asked to bring a friend along with her. Marianne called for a reservation for four. They pulled into the marina and parked, trotting to the payment booth of a cruise company called Cold Mill.

Leslie was already there, sitting at a picnic table with a woman Marianne didn't know, a tall, slim brunette with curly hair. They approached and Marianne gave Leslie a hug, then Leslie kneeled and pulled Stella in for one, too. Leslie introduced, "Marianne, Stella, this is my good friend, Rita. She's visiting Hank and I at the Old Gray Barn. She's from West Virginia. Rita, this is Marianne, Hank's daughter, and our granddaughter, Stella."

Happy conversation bubbled between the four females. Greetings made, they made their way to the booth to get their tickets. Marianne smiled at the woman working. "Three adults, one child." Marianne handed over her credit card and studied the tickets when the woman handed them to her. "Cold Mill. Strange name for a company that relies on warm, sunny weather. Sounds more like something you'd find in Alaska."

The woman said, "My husband and I own the cruise company. We named it that because it cost us a cold mill — a million dollars — to be able to leave our jobs up north, buy our first boat and get this business going. Now, we've been here five years and have four boats. Life is good."

The ladies laughed and boarded the boat. They found four seats near the back, figuring the dolphins would be most viewable from there. The sun, hidden behind clouds the last few days, was making a glorious reappearance today. Marianne took off her sweatshirt, put her longish hair up in a rubber band and put on her sunglasses. The ladies chatted and got to know each other while Stella wandered the boat, looking for all the best dolphin-watching locations.

The ship took off, accompanied by the microphoned chatter of the captain. As they motored through the water in search of the dolphins' playgrounds, Leslie said quietly to Marianne, "How are things progressing between you and Tom?"

Marianne shrugged. "No better, really. We've grown so distant from each other. I've never felt that way before in our marriage. We live in the same house, but we're on opposites sides of this issue. As a result, we seem to avoid talking to each other. We could be living 1000 miles apart, for the amount of togetherness we have."

Leslie grabbed the hand of Rita who was sitting beside her. "Rita could tell you about distance in a marriage."

Rita shrugged and nodded. "It sucks."

Leslie chuckled. "Rita and her husband sometimes only get to see each other a few times a year."

Marianne gasped. "Why?"

Rita leaned forward on her seat so she could get closer to the conversation. "My husband is in the Army Reserves. Sometimes he'll be home for years at a time, serving his commitment only in the summers and an occasional weekend. But when the US went to war with Iraq and the troops were growing short, he was deployed overseas to fight. Over the last five years he's been deployed three times. The first one was six months, but they got longer from there. Once he'd just gotten home, settled in, started back to his regular job, and got deployed again."

"How awful!" Marianne breathed.

"It was insane. He's home right now, has been for several months. There isn't as much need now, so I'm hopeful his deployments might be done. But there are no guarantees, of course. And he loves it. I couldn't take it away from him, although I want to. It means too much to him."

"But it sure makes it hard on you when he's gone."

"Yes. We've gone through our fair share of problems with our son, Nathan. Much of it has been while his dad was overseas. The Army wives' code is to try to handle all the problems at home on their own. Keep their soldier focused on the battlefield. Being distracted by a family problem could cost him his life."

Marianne blinked into Rita's resolute face. "Oh, wow. You're so strong, Rita."

"When I met your stepmom, I wasn't dealing with it very well. In fact, I was about at the end of my rope. Leslie really helped me see that in my attempts to help my young adult son, I was actually making it worse. And by not confiding or sharing with my husband, it was driving this unintentional wedge between us. In addition to being a thousand miles away."

Leslie looked at Marianne and gave her a grim smile.

"You and your husband are a team, no matter if you're getting along right now or not," Rita said. "You have a daughter to raise. That's an important job."

"And a business to run," Marianne added.

"So, fight against the wedge. You're feeling distance in your marriage, but just realize that other wives know what real distance is." She reached over and patted Marianne's hand. "I don't know what your situation is, and please don't think I'm trying to trivialize it or say that mine is worse because my husband's a soldier. That's not my intent. But what I am saying is, there are thousands, probably millions of women out there who would love to have their husbands home with them. Don't overlook the joy and beauty of being together and doing your best to work through your problems."

Marianne studied Rita's face. "Thank you. Thank you very much."

Stella ran over, pointing out the back of the boat. "There it is, Mommy! The first dolphin!" Sure enough, skimming the waves just under the water was the glistening, shiny gray back of a dolphin. They watched it a few seconds before it exploded out of the water, exposing its beautiful form to the boatload of excited tourists.

Stella laughed. "It looks so happy, doesn't it, Mommy?"

Marianne gazed at the animal before it landed back into the water, preparing to jump again. "Yes, baby. It sure does."

Chapter Twelve

Tom hung up the phone, jotted down a note on the pad behind the guest desk and looked up. His father-in-law was passing through the Inn's great room, a pencil in one hand and a stack of blueprint pages in the other. "Hi, Hank."

Hank looked up. "Oh, hi Tom."

"Whatcha got there?"

Hank took a detour and laid the stack of drawings on the guest desk. "Designs of the sets for River City. Marianne tell you I'm responsible for building the stage and sets?"

Tom nodded and refrained from rolling his eyes. Marianne was dead set on moving forward with the dinner theater idea, regardless of his concerns about the endeavor. And now she'd made it a whole family affair. Her dad building the sets, her stepmom directing. If this plan failed, she'd be in good company. He just hoped it wouldn't cost the Inn a lot of money. He realized his father-in-law was looking at him, awaiting his reaction to the drawings. He smiled. "Very nice."

Hank collected them again, rolled them up and shoved them under his arm. He faced the door, then turned and looked at Tom. "Hey, you busy?"

Tom gazed around the desk and shrugged. "Not particularly."

"Want to do some crabbing with me?"

Crabbing? In the middle of a work day? "Sure, why not?"

He followed Hank out the door, down the wooden stairs of his Inn and into the sand parking lot. Hank opened up his truck and tossed the designs inside, then, slamming the door, he led Tom to the bed of the pickup. He pulled out the supplies he must've stuck in there earlier in the day: a cooler to store their live catches, a couple collapsible chairs, a Tupperware container of raw chicken for bait, two weighted drop lines and a net. They divvied up the supplies and carried them across the road. There, a saltwater marsh was the perfect home for the blue claw crab. A ten foot wooden pier, about two feet wide, belonged to the Inn and the men headed down it, stopping almost at the end.

Tom and Hank got to work securing pieces of chicken onto the hook, connecting to the rope line. A metal ball weight was tied to the end of the line, designed to pull the bait down and not let it float up to the top of the water. Soon, the lines were prepared, and they took a step and tossed the line about twelve feet in the water. They watched the rope dive deeper and deeper into the waves.

They settled into their folding chairs, holding onto their lines. Hank removed his ball cap with one hand and wiped his brow with his forearm.

"So, what do you think about this idea of Marianne's," Tom broached, "this dinner theater idea? Do you think Pawleys Island people will enjoy something like that?"

Hank leaned his head on the back of the chair. "I think she's done the research. If she's convinced it'll work, then so am I. She's pretty smart, you know."

Tom nodded. "Yeah. She sure is."

After about ten minutes, they both stood and tugged on their lines, slowly, slowly. Once their bait was visible, and it was clear there were no crabs attached. They pulled the bait out, looking for chomp marks. Nothing yet. They each took a step in a different direction and tossed them in again, letting the blue waves swallow them up.

They chatted about baseball and Hank's work projects and the health of Tom's parents. After a second check, Hank's line had a crab going after the chicken. Leaving the crab a foot or so under the water, Hank grabbed the net and lowered it in behind the crab. In one swift motion, he whooshed the net towards the crab, captured it within, pulled it out of the water and into the cooler. Tom gave him a high five.

Hank prepared new bait on his line and started over again. During the next wait period, he said, "You can tell me to mind my own business, but I hear you're struggling some."

Tom blinked and waited.

"With Jeremy? And his role in your family."

Tom let out a quick rush of air. "Hank, I'm not sure I want to …"

Hank shook his head. "Okay, okay. I'm not goin' to make you talk about it. I just thought I'd offer, if you need an ear to listen, I'd be willing to."

Tom took that opportunity to stand and pull his line out slowly. Another no-go, so he tossed it back in and settled into his chair. A few moments of quiet went by. He'd always enjoyed his father-in-law. He was a man of few words, but deep thoughts, and he tended to give good advice. So, he ventured out with, "Marianne tell you about our disagreement?"

Hank moved his lips into a grimace. "Yeah, a little. If that's what you want to call it."

Tom scoffed. "Yeah, it's more than a disagreement. It's a stalemate."

Hank nodded.

Another minute or two went by. The sun beat down, and sweat dripped down Tom's back but it didn't bother him. Summer was coming and he was happy to see the sun. "I'd say this thing is throwing us for a loop, Hank. She and I have never been this far apart from each other. In, uh, our stance on an issue." Or, for that matter, physically or emotionally. But that wasn't something he wanted to go into with his wife's father.

"Allow a few words of advice from a man who's been married way longer than he was single. It's important to do what's right. But it's not important to always get your way. And sometimes what your wife thinks is right, is just gonna have to do. "

"You're saying, find a compromise."

"I believe you have two choices. You either find a way to get over this, or you'll destroy your relationship. And I know neither of you want that."

Tom creased his forehead in frustration. "You really think it's come to that? You think this silly problem has the power to destroy our marriage?"

Hank looked at him. "It ain't silly to her. Not by a long shot."

Tom drew in a deep breath and let it out slowly. "I love her, as much if not more than I did on the day I married her. I refuse to let this put an end to us."

"Then I suggest you get your negotiation skills out, brush 'em off and put them to use. Neither of you is going to get your way entirely. You have to work together and get past this. Make it work. No use being right if you end up alone, now is there?"

Tom lifted a hand and wiped the perspiration off his lip. He looked over at Hank, slouched in his bag chair. "I thought you were going to stick up for your son."

"No. This ain't about Jeremy. Not really. It's about you and Marianne. It makes no difference what another couple would do to resolve it. You're facing a challenge in your marriage and you need to work it out in a way that you both can live with."

In his unassuming way, his father-in-law had given him something to think about. They crabbed for another two hours, and ultimately went home with a dozen crabs.

* * *

A few weeks later, the Seaside Inn was a bustle of creative endeavor. Emma sat on the back porch with her laptop, putting the finishing touches on her abridged version of *The Music Man* script.

Hank was in the dining room, sawing and hammering, installing the stage. Marianne wanted the cast, once chosen, to rehearse there. The presence of the stage and sets would also draw interest from her guests and hopefully entice them to order tickets, once the website was available.

Leslie was holding informal auditions in the great room. A teacher at the local grade school, Leslie had loads of useful contacts. Because the play's cast featured a large number of school-age children, Leslie had distributed flyers to her teacher friends and encouraged them to talk it up big at school. As a result, she had a steady stream of kids interested in starring in the play. Because Leslie had made friends with teachers at the junior high and high school as well, she'd recruited a rehearsal pianist and a music teacher to direct the music, as well as the donation of a bunch of band instruments from the schools' collections that were vital to the plotline.

Things were progressing, they were coming along. When the last child had sung her little heart out, Marianne watched Leslie wrap up the audition, hand out contact sheets to all the parents and bid them all off. Then she came over to where Marianne sat on the couch and plopped herself down, exhaling.

"We've got the entire cast filled except two."

"Wow! That's great," Marianne replied. "Which two?"

Leslie laughed. "No. Let's savor our successes for a moment. We've got the entire children's cast selected. We've got all our townspeople, including our barbershop quartet. We've got Winthrop and most of the key roles."

Marianne smiled, reached over and pulled Leslie into a hug. "Great job, director."

"We could start rehearsals this week with the kids, start teaching dance moves and songs."

"Super."

"But," Leslie said.

"Here's the but."

"We don't have our leads. We need a Marian the Librarian and a Professor Harold Hill."

Marianne nodded, pondering. "Do you know anyone from school who does community theater and could pull it off?"

Leslie sighed. "Not really. Everyone who has auditioned so far, I've slotted into smaller roles. We need a real standout for Marian, and an equally excellent Professor Hill. They carry so much of the show. It's okay to use talented amateurs for the townspeople and kids. But we need professional-caliber talent for those two roles. Otherwise, the entire endeavor could be a flop."

"Okay."

"The other thing is, even though the community theater in Myrtle is helping sponsor us, we're also competing with them. They're doing their spring musical at the same time, so anyone in the surrounding area who can sing and dance and likes to perform, will be auditioning there."

Marianne waited for a feeling of stress to overcome her at this huge problem. Breathlessness, a racing pulse. She had a great deal at stake, and had invested a lot in this project. Tom was against it, and if she failed to deliver a high quality, not to mention profitable production, he would have every reason to say, "I told you so."

But the only emotion she felt was excitement. This wasn't a problem — it was an opportunity. A chance to not only make this show good, but to push it to great.

"Don't you worry about it, Leslie. I'm going to take care of this. Move forward with rehearsals. I'll find our leads and make sure you approve. And they're going to be great."

Marianne went to the kitchen and fetched two glasses of iced tea, then went through the Inn to the back porch. Emma sat on a rocking chair, her feet propped up on a table, her knees bent and her laptop in her lap. Her fingers danced over the keyboard and she didn't notice Marianne until she sat down beside her.

"Oh, hi."

"Hi. How's it going? I thought you could use some refreshment."

"Thanks." Emma accepted the glass and took a long sip. "It's going well. I've ended up cutting almost an hour of material from the stage play version. Did you know there are fourteen musical numbers in Act 1 and another eleven in Act 2?" She smiled.

"No, wow."

"So I'm cutting it by reducing the songs that we do keep to less verses, and then axing some of the songs that are incidental to the plot. If I do it right, the audience won't even notice the changes. They'll just enjoy a swift production of one of their favorite musicals without having to sit through over three hours of performance."

Marianne took a sip of her iced tea. "Well, I'm sure you're doing it right."

"Dinner theaters are unique because the actors actually serve the meal, then perform onstage while the guests eat. At intermission, they run out and clear the dishes, and serve dessert. They really work hard. But I suppose the guests tip them extra well if they're enjoying their performance."

Emma tapped on her keyboard a few more strokes, then closed her laptop lid. "I estimate I'll be done in the next day or two, then I want to actually time it — read through the whole thing and sing the songs with the timer on. Then I'll turn it over to you. Does that fit your time restraints?"

Marianne nodded. "Perfect."

"Did I ever tell you that *The Music Man* was the first live musical I ever went to? Yep, it was at the community theater in Myrtle Beach, and one of my classmates played Winthrop. We were probably in junior high. He was great, and from then on I always sort of regarded him as a celebrity. It was a magical experience. It's when I got the bug for theater. I don't act or sing, but I am one of the most enthralled observers in the whole audience."

"Magical," Marianne mused. "I hope we can introduce a few people to the magic of live theater with our production."

Emma looked down at her lap and said softly, "It meant a lot to me that you asked me to adapt the script. That was nice of you."

"Nice of me! It was nice of you to use your talents and your time to help out."

Emma shook her head. "I'm happy to do it. But that's not really what I meant. I'm talking about what happened to Stella and … my dad's role in it."

"Emma," Marianne said and reached over and gripped her hand.

Emma went on. "I feel so awful that my dad did that. I still can't imagine what he was thinking. I guess he had slipped beyond the realm of sane, and I never noticed it."

"It's not your fault, sweetie."

"I agree it's not my fault that he took her, but maybe if I weren't so wrapped up in my own life, I would've noticed signs that he was in trouble. So that I could've discovered it before he did something so crazy and put Stella's life in danger."

"You can't blame yourself."

Emma turned in her seat so she was facing Marianne head-on. "I was falling in love, Marianne. With your brother. And because of that, I couldn't see outside my own happiness. I missed the fact that my father was losing it."

Marianne smiled. It was the first time Emma had confided in her that she was falling in love with Jeremy. If life turned out this way, she'd be happy to have Emma for a sister-in-law. "Oh Emma, I'm so happy for you and Jeremy. But honestly, you did a lot to help your father. You tried to convince him to go to Alcoholics Anonymous. You encouraged him to control his drinking. You weren't just in a cloud, in love. You were helping your family. And don't forget, you helped find our little girl."

Emma gazed into Marianne's eyes. "Thank you for saying that. But I know Tom doesn't agree with you. I hope you don't mind, Jeremy has shared with me a little bit about your disagreement."

Marianne let her eyes wander. "Yes, we're having a hard time with this. He and I are so far apart on this particular topic, I don't know how we'll ever come to a compromise."

"He doesn't want Jeremy around. He thinks Jeremy presents a danger to Stella."

Marianne nodded. "Of course, that's ridiculous."

"He's just being a protective daddy."

"But if he thinks I'll agree to disowning my brother, I really don't see how we can move forward in our marriage."

"I understand. I'm sorry for pushing into something so personal."

"Actually, I need to talk about it and don't have a lot of prospects."

They finished their tea while looking out at the ocean, the cool breeze reaching them through the screen windows.

Emma set her glass down. "I better get going. I'm helping Jeremy plan his store's Grand Opening. He's a talented wood worker, but awful at marketing."

"Don't I know it! And how exciting. What do you have planned?"

"Balloons, food, champagne, special discounts and giveaways. All the stuff he wishes he could ignore."

Marianne chuckled. "Keep on him. I think that store could be a real success for him."

Emma stood and Marianne followed her into the Inn. "Oh," Emma said and turned, "I wanted to share with you a few ideas I had for promoting the dinner theater. Once it's getting ready to go live, I could see if I could do a story for the magazine. We'd have to come up with an inspirational slant to the production, but I'm sure we'll have no trouble with that. Also, I have contacts at the newspaper so I'm sure I can get us some free mentions there too."

Marianne gave her a hug and bid her farewell.

* * *

Late that night, after she'd put Stella to bed, Marianne pulled out her laptop and settled on the couch in the apartment. On a whim, she went to Google and typed in, "websites for actors and actresses." To her amazement, a long list of links were presented to her. Although, on second thought, she didn't know why she was amazed. You could Google anything.

She researched the sites and discovered that there were many that offered exactly what she was looking for — a way to connect with actors and actresses looking for work. Some listed performers looking for work. Marianne could scan their headshots, resumes and compensation requirements. Others listed the show that needed talent, so performers could express their interest. After scanning both types of sites for a half hour, Marianne decided it couldn't hurt to try both in order to cast her Marian and Harold Hill.

Many of the sites required a payment to either list the show, or to review the actors looking for work. Marianne decided to go ahead and invest a nominal amount in order to get in touch with the right people.

"What are you doing?"

Tom had wandered in and Marianne hadn't even noticed. Her first impulse was to draw back, keep him from seeing what she was up to. But that was wrong. He may not be an active partner with her in this production, or even support what she was doing. But she wasn't doing anything behind his back. In fact, it was probably time for one of those periodic progress updates.

"Have a seat, Tom."

He gave her an inquisitive look but did as she asked.

"I want to give you an update on the dinner theater." She paused, waiting for a roll of his eyes or some other sign of disapproval, but to his credit, he didn't do it. "Things are going really well. In an effort to keep you informed, I'll run through the progress made, as well as the challenge we're facing."

Tom nodded.

"I've secured a number of volunteers who are working on the dinner theater project for no pay."

Tom's eyebrows shut up. "Well, that's good."

Marianne smirked. "We've cast about 90% of the parts with local talent, and we've adapted the script to shorten it. We have a director and a music director. We have costumes and our stage has been built. We have props available to us. Rehearsals will start any day now."

As she spoke, his mouth dropped. "Oh, my gosh."

Ignoring him, she continued, "My dad is ready to start building the sets, and I'll help him with painting. We have committed free advertising in *Seminal* magazine and the Myrtle Beach newspaper. I'm going to work on enhancing our Inn's website with information about the dinner theater and add a link to purchase tickets."

He shook his head in wonder. "Unbelievable. You've made so much progress in less than a month."

Marianne nodded. "When I put my mind to something, there's little that can stop me."

He scoffed. "Don't I know it." He ran a hand over his eyes, suddenly looking tired. "So you mentioned a challenge."

"Yes." She turned the laptop screen toward him. "Everything we've done so far has been low budget. We're lucky that I have very supportive friends and family, and lots of community folks who love performing. But we can't be cheap when it comes to the leading lady and man. We need to invest in musical theater professionals to really pull this off and make it a successful show."

Tom sighed. "That sounds expensive."

"Like I said, we've gotten off easy so far. We've barely spent anything. This is where we need to make our investment. Spend money to make money."

He laid his head back on the couch. "How much?"

"I was just researching that. I found these websites where you can advertise your show and the roles that are open. I searched on dinner theaters in vacation towns to get an idea of the going rate. What's really great is we can offer them free room and board, then bring down the weekly pay rate. Not all dinner theaters have that going for them."

"How many rooms?"

"No more than two."

Tom shrugged. "Seems doable. Then how much in paycheck?"

Marianne turned back to the laptop. "Let me find at least four or five in similar locations as ours and I'll come up with a price range. To draw top talent, I think we need to offer pay at the top of the range. Make our job stand out in the crowd."

Tom stared at her for a silent moment. "You're impressive, you know that?"

Marianne frowned.

"You have no experience with this whatsoever, other than what you've dove into over the last month. And look at you — you're a pro now. You know exactly what you're doing, you've gotten tons of people involved, you've gotten almost your whole list of tasks done. You're good, baby."

Despite the fact that if he'd had his way, he would've halted the entire production, it was good to hear the compliment. "Thanks." She shrugged. "You ain't seen nothing yet."

"That won't surprise me at all."

She turned back to her laptop with a smile. As she concentrated on her research, she realized he hadn't moved away. In fact, just the opposite. He was getting closer.

He leaned in and placed his lips on her neck. He knew kissing her neck was one of her favorite things in the world. He always made her shiver, which made her yearn for his heat and closeness.

How easy it would be to sink back into familiar intimacy with her husband. Part of her didn't see any reason not to. They were married, committed to each other, drawn together by God to serve each other's needs.

She pulled back. "Tom, no."

He said in a husky tone, "Sorry, am I distracting you from your work?"

She took a deep breath and let it out. "It's not that. I can do this anytime."

He looked at her and grinned, his white teeth sparkling in the darkened room. He reached for her laptop and started to move it to the coffee table in front of her.

"I love you, Tom, but I can't be intimate with you until we come to an agreement about your Jeremy ultimatum. It wouldn't feel true. I can't make love to you while inside, I'm furious with you."

Tom sighed and leaned back on the couch, creating a little distance from her. "We seemed to be getting along a little better and I thought …"

"You thought … I would just forget the fact that you want to cut my brother out of our lives? Just because you gave me a compliment about how well the show preparations are going? Which, by the way, you were against, as well? No. We've got a long ways to go before we can move from pleasantries to intimacy."

Tom stood and walked to the other side of the room, leaning against the wall so he could look at her. "Honey, I mentioned in our therapy session about my dad and my brother, Rod."

She nodded.

"I'm just trying to avoid making the same mistakes in my family that my dad made in his. You realize that, right? My dad let my brother get away with too much harm and destruction and we all paid the price with grieving and sadness. I want our family to flourish. I want us to be happy. Sort of like tearing off a bandage, it may hurt to cut ties with Jeremy at first. But in the long run, we'll get over it faster, heal, and live a happy life, free from drama. I guess you can't see that right now, you're so close to it. But that's all I'm trying to do, learn from my own parents."

Marianne picked up her laptop again. "Your motives are pure, but your methods are just plain wrong. There are other ways that don't involve ripping my heart out."

He flinched at her choice of words.

"But until you start exploring some of those options, you and I have a problem."

Chapter Thirteen

The next few days, Marianne stayed busy with her cyber-duties. She narrowed down her actor/actress search sites to three. She posted the details on all three: *The Music Man* Dinner Theater at the Seaside Inn in Pawleys Island, South Carolina. She had no idea if she'd get any takers. The sites offered four options for location: LA, Broadway, off-Broadway and regional. Probably couldn't get away with listing their production as off-Broadway. How far off was off? She listed it as regional and was as open and honest as possible so she would only get interested applicants.

She consulted with Leslie, who had now started rehearsals with the support cast. Two hours a night, one day with the kids, the next with adults. She'd mapped out a whole schedule with the total rehearsal timeframe lasting six weeks. Based on that tentative timeline, Marianne could work on the Dinner Theater pages for the Inn website. She researched a dozen other dinner theater sites and designed some pages that she thought were attractive and fun. Once she was satisfied that they looked professional and inviting, she published them to the web, along with the ticket sales page. She could always adjust the show dates later if they weren't quite right.

Their hard work was paying off and it was getting closer. Her heart pounded just thinking about it. Despite the conflict this decision had caused with Tom, she was glad she had moved forward with the idea. She loved stretching her wings and trying something new. She couldn't imagine God would want her living her life stuck in what was tried and true and safe.

Later, she took a shopping list from Leslie, and headed out to the store. As if on its own accord, the car rerouted and headed to Jeremy's furniture store. She assumed he'd be in there working, even though it wasn't open yet, still working and building inventory for his Grand Opening.

She pulled into the strip mall lot and parked. She tapped on the glass of his front door. He was inside, just as she suspected, working on a wooden piece. He looked up, waved, and grabbed a cloth to wipe his hands. He headed over to the door and opened it.

She stepped in beside him and pulled him into a hug. He tensed at first, and then his shoulders relaxed and he abided the display of affection from his little sister. When she pulled away, she wiped a few tears from her eyes.

"Oh, sis," he said with a chuckle.

"I can't help it! I haven't seen you in ages. It's bad enough we had to go so long without seeing you regularly. I can't stand the thought that we're right in the same town and I never see you."

He nodded and gestured to the bookshelf he'd been working on. She followed him back over to it, where he resumed his work. "You're really not supposed to be here."

"Says who?"

He glanced up with eyebrows raised. "Your husband."

"He's not the boss of me," she said with laughter in her voice.

Jeremy chuckled, applying stain on the bookcase with even strokes of his brush. "But seriously. I don't want you guys fighting over me. Relationships are hard enough. Save your fights for something more important."

She got closer to him and smacked his shoulder with her fist.

"Hey!" She'd thrown him off-balance and he almost dropped his paintbrush.

"You deserved that. You *are* important."

He smirked and kept working. Marianne looked around and found a wooden chair close by, and pulled it over. She sat. "I have to admit this argument is the worst we've ever had. I just can't believe we're so far apart on this one."

Jeremy's face tightened. "Don't fight because of me, sis. He's a good man and he loves you."

"But he's dead-wrong about this. You're my brother and my family is very important to me. I can't accept this ultimatum just because he's a good man. He has to see the error of his ways."

Jeremy let out a deep breath and kept staining.

"Let's change the subject. Let's talk about you. And Emma."

As he stained the bookcase, his whole body got into it. Long strokes of his arms, his torso moving in rhythm, his hair, a little long now, dropping over his eyes, bobbing in time. She detected a slight upturn of his lips.

"Things going well?" she asked nonchalantly.

"Yes."

"Good to hear." An unbidden grin popped on her face. She was thrilled to hear her brother was in a relationship with a woman, someone he could eventually love and settle down with. But she knew better than to pry. Push him too hard and he'd back down and not tell her anything.

"How's she feeling about her dad and all?"

"She's heartbroken. She can't believe he did what he did, and especially that she didn't detect the start of his breakdown. And she regrets her role in this whole mess."

"Her role?"

"Yeah. If she hadn't met me, and we hadn't started dating, her dad wouldn't have been pushed over the edge, emotionally."

Marianne shrugged. "Yeah but, from what I understand, her family's life wasn't a party before she met you. Her dad was unemployed, unmotivated and drank too much. Her mom worked too hard to support them the best she could. Not exactly a Norman Rockwell moment." Marianne quieted and studied Jeremy, mesmerized by his talent with the wood and the beautiful result. "This is gorgeous, by the way."

"Thanks. I'll either sell it as a standalone or I did make other pieces to sell as a set. This stand-up book case, a desk and a wooden chair." He stopped his staining to gesture vaguely to another grouping of wooden pieces a ways away.

"Hard to believe you have so much inventory now. You've been working your butt off, haven't you?"

He smiled and nodded.

"And to think that after Emma's dad set the storage shed on fire, you only had a handful of pieces left."

"I'm hoping for a solid Grand Opening. The key is having plenty of pieces people can put their hands and eyes on."

"I'm proud of you," she said simply.

Jeremy scoffed. He was never good at taking praise, but lately more than ever.

"Making your dreams come true." She made an effort to control the emotion in her voice, but he'd heard the catch, and rolled his eyes at her.

"Sis," he said.

"So, when's Grand Opening?" she asked, changing the subject.

"I'm thinking about two weeks. Emma's helping with the marketing. She's got big ideas. Fortunately, she leaves me mostly out of it so I can build furniture."

"You know she's been helping me too, with the Dinner Theater."

He reached a stopping point with the bookcase and set his brush down. He looked at her with interest. "Yeah, I want to hear about that. Come back to the kitchen with me."

She followed him to the back of the store, carefully dodging gorgeous showroom pieces, trying to restrain herself from stopping and studying each one. In a tiny room in the back containing a stove, refrigerator, microwave, sink, table and chairs, he washed his hands thoroughly. When he was finished, he opened the fridge and pulled out two cans of cola, opened them both and gave her one.

When he sat across from her, she finally had his undivided attention. She told him about her Dinner Theater idea, how Tom thought it was too risky with no guarantee of profitability, and all the progress made so far. She praised Emma for her work abridging the script, filled him in on Leslie's efforts with selecting and rehearsing the cast, and their dad's progress with building the stage and sets.

"A real family affair," he said with a smile.

She nodded. "It's been fun. I just need really stellar actors for the two leads. It could flop without them. And I need to sell some tickets."

"What can I do?" he asked, and then he lowered his head.

She knew he'd offered naturally, before remembering the constraints Tom had placed on him. She patted his hand. "How about I print up some flyers and you can hand them out at your Grand Opening?"

"Absolutely. I'd be happy to do that."

She stayed long enough to finish her soft drink. She said her good-byes and Jeremy walked her to the door. Sadly, she leaned into him, and he wrapped an arm around her shoulders. Close to her ear, he murmured, "It'll all work out, Marianne. You'll see."

She pulled back. "Do you pray, Jeremy?"

"I sure do."

"Then pray for my family. Pray for Tom and me. Because I can't live like this for long, with a wedge between us. It's just not in me."

He nodded his agreement, pain evident in the lines on his face, and squeezed her hand. He waved as she left and locked the door behind her, back to work.

* * *

The next few weeks became a whirlwind of dinner theater activity. The sound of joyful music rehearsals filled the Inn's dining room every evening. The music brought happiness to Marianne's heart because of the familiarity of the songs and the fun the kids were having learning them. Inn guests ventured back to the dining room after the dinner meal to pull up chairs and watch the rehearsals.

Staging and dialogue rehearsals were coming along too. They were blessed with a fairly experienced adult cast. Many of them had done musical theater in high school, or had followed their interest into their adult years, performing at the community theater. Marianne was amazed by their gracefulness and comfort on stage, since this was a talent she'd never had. Sure, she could organize and control. But she could never get up there and perform.

Checking their website results became an obsession. Multiple times every day, whenever she was near a computer, she checked to see if any actors had shown interest in coming to work for them. And she checked to see if any tickets were sold.

So far, a big fat zero on both counts, which would incite, multiple times a day, a wave of panic to rush over her. What if they went to all this work, and had gotten this far, but couldn't cast the leads? And what if no one came to see them? Tom would give her an "I told you so" that she would fully deserve. Which about killed her.

She needed to prove the validity of this idea. She *needed* it to be a success. She *needed* her idea to dig them out of the financial hole they were in.

So, she went back to planning. Where else could she advertise the dinner theater? Where could she stack flyers? Where could she advertise online that would draw in the audience? How could she reach out and find just the right Marian and Harold?

* * *

Opening Day for Jeremy's furniture store arrived, along with a beautiful late-spring gift of sunshine and warmth. Marianne showered and dressed, a happy smile on her face. She selected a cute dress for Stella as well, wanting her to look her best.

She hated the grip on her heart at the thought of taking Stella to Jeremy's Opening. She supposed she should at least inform her husband of her plans. When she encountered him in the Inn's great room, she said, "Today is Jeremy's Grand Opening. He's got a beautiful day for it."

Tom looked up from the ledger he was reviewing behind the guest desk. "What?"

"Jeremy's furniture store. He's been working hard building inventory pieces. Today's the day he opens to the public."

"Oh." Tom looked back to his numbers.

"I'm going there for his celebration, and I'm taking Stella."

Tom's head shot back up. Marianne lifted her hand, a literal STOP sign. "Tom, I can guarantee you that Stella will not be in danger going to Jeremy's Grand Opening celebration along with, hopefully, hundreds of other people. I want her to support her uncle in his success and it'll be nice for Jeremy to see her, too. It's been well over a month since they've seen each other."

Tom clenched his mouth shut and she imagined that he was physically stopping his words of protest from escaping.

"I'm letting you know, but I'm not asking your permission," she said, and turned back to the apartment.

A half hour later, Marianne and Stella were on their way. The minute she pulled into the parking lot, she grinned at the festiveness. A huge banner draped across the doorway of Jeremy's store, proclaiming "SALE!! IN CELEBRATION OF HARRISON DESIGNS GRAND OPENING." Smaller banners were displayed in the windows of each neighboring business in the strip mall. "Look at that, Stella! Isn't that exciting?"

Stella squealed and pointed at the colorful banners and balloons. Marianne noticed that although they were thirty minutes prior to the opening, there was a good little crowd of cars in the lot, and about a dozen people lined up at the door. Her heart rushed with gratitude and excitement for her brother's well-earned success.

They approached the door and Marianne ran into someone she knew while Stella darted through the small crowd to get a good spot to see inside. Marianne made sure she knew where her daughter was, then turned to chat with one of the mothers of a boy in Stella's class. She was explaining that Jeremy was her brother when she heard Stella scream, "Mommy! Mommy! Oh my gosh, come look!"

"Excuse me," she said and pushed to the front of the gathered folks. "What is it, baby?" she asked when she reached Stella, who was jumping in place and pointing at the plate-glass window.

Inside, Jeremy was kneeling on one knee in front of Emma, holding out a small box on his palm. Marianne gasped. "Oh Stella, do you know what this means?"

"No! What's in that box?" But the little girl knew it was important and exciting, judging from the way she was now hopping and holding her hand over her mouth.

Marianne peered through the window. She couldn't see exactly what was in the box, but she could bet it was a velvet box from a jeweler containing a diamond solitaire ring. And it was unmistakable the intent behind it.

Emma snatched the box from his hand and pulled the ring from it, then handed it back to Jeremy, who slipped it on her left ring finger. He started to rise but Emma pushed his shoulders down, saying something to him which Marianne couldn't hear. But he must've liked what he heard because he stood and lifted Emma, twirling her around in a circle, their lips joined.

"Oh Stella," she breathed. "Uncle Jeremy just asked Emma to marry him!"

"Really? How do you know?"

"That's how it's done, sweetie. Man on one knee, a ring on her finger, and a big happy kiss." Those tears that had been prevalent for weeks hit her eyes again, but this time they were for pure happiness.

She stared through the window, a happy smile on her face, her heart exploding. Eventually, the two lovebirds must've realized they had an audience because they turned to the crowd. They'd been oblivious during the proposal, but now, it was time to work. Jeremy gave Emma a last kiss and strode to the door, unlocking it and throwing it open. "Welcome, folks. Welcome to Harrison Designs. We have lots of sales going on, so come on in and take a look."

She let him direct his anxious customers in the door, then she pulled him aside and gave him a huge embrace. "Jeremy! Congratulations! I assume she said yes?"

He laughed, a big, unencumbered, happy smile covering his face. "She said she loves me. And she wants to stick around for a future with me." He noticed Stella and squatted down to receive her hug as well. "Hi cupcake. Great to see you, sweetheart."

"And the wedding?"

He rose. "No wedding yet. This wasn't an engagement. Just a commitment. Look, sis. I gotta get busy. Go check out the ring." And off he went.

Marianne turned in a circle till she spotted Emma. She grabbed Stella's hand and practically pulled her over. When Emma saw her, she beamed. "Congratulations!"

Emma laughed. "You saw that?"

"We sure did. And what's this about it wasn't an engagement? It sure looked like a marriage proposal, which leads to an engagement."

Emma smiled and held out her left hand, palm down. A stunning red ruby surrounded by small diamonds rested in a gold band. It sparkled in the bright lights of the showroom, and matched the beautiful smile of its wearer.

"Let me see!" Stella urged.

Emma laughed and lifted Stella up and held her so she could get a close look. As Stella studied the ring, Emma turned to Marianne. "He's old-fashioned. He doesn't want to plan a wedding until he's financially stable and has a future to offer me. But I'm not concerned about that. He's the man I love. We can build all this together. I don't really need to wait."

Marianne leaned her cheek in close to Emma's, squeezing her as best she could while she still held Stella. "I'm so happy for you both. You know that, right?"

"I sure do. Thanks, Marianne."

With that, Emma disappeared into the crowd of people who were there to make Jeremy's dream come true.

* * *

They spent a good hour at the store, talking to customers, watching Jeremy and Emma ring up sales and take orders for custom-built projects. With news that the TV camera crew was coming later, Marianne and Stella took off. The Grand Opening was a huge success. Jeremy and Emma had worked hard and it had paid off. Jeremy's business was off and running.

The excitement over the proposal floated over them the whole way home, and Stella couldn't chatter about anything else. In her mind, Emma was a princess and Uncle Jeremy her doting prince. This was the closest thing to a fairy tale Stella had ever experienced.

Which is why, the first words out of her mouth once she saw her daddy were, "Guess what Daddy? Uncle Jeremy and Emma are going to get married! He gave her a ring and put it on her finger! He proposed on one knee!"

Marianne beamed at her daughter, the little girl's excitement contagious. Until she looked back at her husband. She supposed she didn't expect him to be blissful at the news. But she certainly didn't expect the anger that was plain on his face.

"That's great, sweetie," he said in a strained voice.

Stella went on, "Emma's going to be a beautiful bride, isn't she Daddy? And Uncle Jeremy will be the handsome groom in the black tuxedo!"

"Yes," he said. "Now listen sweetheart, why don't you go get changed for the beach? I'll take you out to dig, how's that?"

She shrieked her pleasure at that suggestion, and darted back to the apartment.

"They're getting married?" he said with short, even words.

"Well, yes. And no."

"What's that mean?"

"In his mind, it wasn't a marriage proposal. He presented her with a ruby ring, not a diamond, and to him, it's more of a commitment."

"Like a promise ring?"

"Yes, exactly."

Tom paused, let out some pent up breath.

"But not to Emma. She loves him, and considers it an engagement ring. She sees no need to wait."

Tom's mouth tightened and he ran his fingers over his lips. He turned toward the apartment and took a few steps, then turned back. "All the more reason to keep Stella away from the both of them."

"What?" Marianne exploded. "What could this possibly have to do with the other?"

"Jeremy will be bound to Slotky forever now."

Marianne shook her head, at a loss for his logic. "Slotky is in jail! He can't get to Stella."

"Prison sentences are temporary, at best. If he gets out — *when* he gets out, now Jeremy's not just dating his daughter. He's married his daughter. Now what's he going to do?"

"Tom, I refuse to let you mar this happy *Harrison* family occasion."

Tom laid his hand on her arm. "Stella stays away from them. You understand? For her own safety."

Marianne's mouth dropped and she pointed at the apartment door. "You heard her! She's more excited about this engagement than I've ever seen her. You can't keep her from all the wedding excitement."

"I can. And I will. And I expect you to honor my wishes on this, even if you don't agree with it."

He stormed to the apartment, and she watched him as if in a daze. This couldn't be happening. It just couldn't.

Chapter Fourteen

The fight with Tom caused a dark haze to settle over her head, difficult to fight through in order to continue with her daily responsibilities. She hated marital spats, always had. But this one was the doozy of all marital fights. The anger in Tom's eyes as he'd dictated his directive about Stella, refusing to let her be a part of Jeremy's wedding … it caused a chill to settle over her unlike any she'd ever known. How could they ever get over this disagreement?

Or was this the beginning of the end? If they couldn't resolve this conflict, how could they possibly stay married? It was too big, too far-reaching. She couldn't support him in his direction, and he obviously couldn't support her in hers. They both had responsibility for Stella's upbringing and safety, and they were at opposite ends of the spectrum.

Tears were never far from her eyes. The smallest little problem resulted in an unwanted eruption of tears, when she knew, in absence of this problem, she wouldn't be fighting them back.

She couldn't live like this. As much as it pained her, she had to be realistic and start considering the possibility of divorcing Tom. It chilled her to the bone to even think about, but there was no way she could survive in a marriage with a man who had lost all her respect.

In a quiet moment at the Inn, she pulled out her Bible again, looking for guidance. God's word made clear His thoughts about divorce:

> Malachi 2:16: "The man who hates and divorces his wife," says the LORD, the God of Israel, "does violence to the one he should protect," says the LORD Almighty. So be on your guard, and do not be unfaithful.
>
> Matthew 19:8: Jesus replied, "Moses permitted you to divorce your wives because your hearts were hard. But it was not this way from the beginning. I tell you that anyone who divorces his wife, except for sexual immorality, and marries another woman commits adultery."

But there was a huge expanse between living the type of marital love that God described in her previous Bible study, and this: an avoidance of divorce. Sure, God wants us to avoid divorce, but how can a couple possibly fulfill God's view of a successful marriage, with an unresolvable wedge between them?

Marianne closed her Bible with more force than she'd meant to, stood and went to find Tom. She didn't have to look far. He was outside, trimming the bushes and greenery in front of the Inn. He looked up at her approach, then his head stubbornly lowered, focusing on the electric trimmer. His jaw clenched with his determination to keep his mouth closed. Anger radiated from him in waves and it didn't take being married to the man to recognize it.

So, he wasn't going to turn the machine off, even though it was obvious she'd come and found him to talk. Fine. She waved her hand in front of his face, then crossed her arms in front of her chest.

Finally, he turned the machine off and said in one terse syllable, "Yes?"

She took a deep breath and let it out. Now that she had his attention, what would she do with it? She hadn't really thought out a plan. "I think it's obvious that our disagreement has taken a turn for the worst."

He nodded.

"So I want to visit the topic of marriage counseling again. Should I call Stephanie's office and get a referral for a couples counselor?"

He shrugged, then shook his head, his gaze going beyond her on the horizon.

Marianne waited for a verbal response but didn't get one. "Or, we could make an appointment with Pastor Gray at church. He knows us both and might be able to add some spiritual insight."

"No." Tom's answer was fast and strong. "Not with Pastor Gray. I don't want him knowing about our troubles."

"Why not?"

He let out a breath and lowered the trimmer to rest on the ground. "I don't know. It's a small town, Marianne. Word gets out. I'd feel uncomfortable around our friends. Might be bad for business."

Marianne wondered how many other lame excuses he could come up with if she let him. "Never mind, then. I'm busy with the dinner theater. I just thought that working on our marriage was a priority to you. Maybe I was wrong."

He stammered but she didn't give him a chance to finalize his thoughts into words. She whirled and stormed back up the stairs to the Inn. Yes, she realized it was childish, but she honestly didn't know how much longer she could take this tension between them. Let him stew and come to her with a suggestion for fixing their marriage.

The best way to get through her day was to keep busy. Which was good, because as the Dinner Theater's opening night approached, there were still a million details to work out. First of which was selling tickets. The ticket sales website had been published for over a week, and not a single ticket had been bought. Trying not to panic, Marianne reasoned: they were new to the theater scene. People wouldn't necessarily be scanning the Inn's website looking for theater opportunities. They needed to link to other theater sites where their customers might be looking. That was her task for today: research other places on the web where she could link their page and draw interest.

She pulled up the Admin section of the ticket sales page, as she'd done every day since it went live. She gasped, then leaned closer to the screen to make sure she was seeing this right.

There were ticket sales! Unlike every other day when it said zero sales, there were now over twenty confirmed purchases to come see their dinner theater.

This thing just got real.

* * *

Marianne sat in the dining room, watching the rehearsals. Leslie and the Music Director called up the traveling salesmen for the opening scene of the show. The actors sat on a make-believe train, bouncing in unison in their seats as the train clacked down the tracks. The song was performed in rhythmic speaking voices all in unison. Words and rhythm and pace, all equally important to pull this challenging number off, all had to be exactly in sync. But they'd rehearsed it numerous times, and the adult actors in the scene were getting it. Marianne's heart raced, loving the quality of the production, *her* production.

At the end of the scene, they had to leave a blank spot for the big reveal of Professor Harold Hill, the con man who was on the train looking for the location of his next con. Because of course, they hadn't cast Harold yet. Or Marian, the local librarian he falls in love with.

Leslie moved them straight from the end of the train number into the first big musical number of the show, "Iowa Stubborn." The townspeople of River City strolled across the stage which, when done, would be decorated with beautifully painted sets featuring the wholesome streets of a typical Iowa town in 1912. They would eventually be dressed in period costumes, the women in long modest long dresses, the men in full suits. This wasn't a dress rehearsal, but the costumes had arrived on loan from the community theater in Myrtle Beach. In fact, the garment bags were heaped in a corner of the dining room and needed to be sorted and passed out to the actors. She reached for her notebook and jotted it down. She and Leslie would have to do that, maybe tomorrow night after practice.

Tom came in, saw her and walked over. He stood beside her chair, his head lifted to the singers on stage. She tried to ignore him, but finally looked up and saw a pleased smile on his face.

When the number completed, Tom applauded and made his way closer to the stage. "Sounds great, sounds great, everyone. Thanks for all your hard work on this. I'm Tom, and my wife Marianne and I own the Inn. This is the first time we've even considered doing a dinner theater, so you guys are part of history being made here. Best of luck, break a leg, and let's all hope for a long run."

He smiled as the cast applauded, showing their appreciation for his supportive message, and he turned and came back to Leslie's table. She fixed him with an eyebrows-up glare.

"What?"

"You vetoed the idea! If it weren't for me being persistent, we wouldn't even be doing the show."

He laughed. "You're right. And in this case, I'm glad you pushed back on me. I wasn't thinking creatively enough. Time to jump outside the box and try something new. They sound really, really good! I take no credit for it. You guys have all worked really hard. Congratulations."

Marianne shook her head. "It's definitely coming along." Behind them, the children launched into a rehearsal of "Seventy-Six Trombones," minus Harold's solo.

"How are ticket sales looking?" Tom asked, always interested in the bottom line.

"Good. Amazingly good. In fact, we're getting consistent reservations, more every day."

"Great." He smiled at her and then ambled out of the dining room.

But it wasn't great, Marianne thought. Well, it *was*. It was great that people were showing interest and reserving their seats for what would hopefully be the best show in town. But it wasn't, because they had no leads. Which made Marianne sweat with panic each time she allowed herself to think about it. Whoever heard of a top-rate production with just the supporting cast? They had to secure their leads, *now*, or else they couldn't proceed with Opening Night as planned. The cast was already over 50% rehearsed. The rate they were going, they would be ready to perform in two weeks.

Marianne sighed and went to find her computer. She'd gotten accustomed to finding no responses to her ad for actors. But it was time for Plan B. If she hadn't gotten a response today, she'd have to think of something else.

She pulled up her email program and scanned through her Inbox. Towards the top, there it was. An email with the Subject Line: Music Man lead role. Her hands shaking, she moved her cursor there and clicked on it. As it opened, she closed her eyes and prayed that it was not just an inquiry. That it was a bona fide, qualified actor who had researched the role, and the location and the terms of the job, and was honestly looking for a chance.

She took a deep breath, let it out and opened her eyes.

The email had only arrived ten minutes ago, and it was from a woman named Roxanne Frazier. It read, "Dear Ms. Mueller, I am writing to express my interest in the role of Marian Paroo in your dinner theater production of *The Music Man*. I have been a member of the Actor's Equity for four years, and I have worked professionally in New York City for three of those four years. I sing, I dance, I act. You name it. I've attached my headshot so you can see if you visualize me in the role. I've also attached my professional resume so you can see everything I've done. But there's something about spending the spring and possibly summer at a seaside inn in a beach town that really speaks to my tired soul. This girl's tired of the city, the traffic, the hustle bustle. I think working in Pawleys Island is exactly what I need."

Marianne immediately clicked on the attachments and stared into the eyes of a beautiful, blonde, fit twenty-something smiling back at her. And read about the accomplishments of this prolific actress over the last few years. She'd done musical theater, not on Broadway, but off-Broadway and even did a four-month stint in a traveling ensemble of *The Wedding Singer*.

And best of all, she was interested!

Without hesitation, she picked up the phone and punched out the number Roxanne had listed in her email. It rang three times and then a harried, "Hello," shouted over the line. In the background, the sound of heavy traffic filled the void, horns honking, voices shouting.

"Hello? Roxanne Frazier?"

"Yes. Who's this? I'm sorry, I can barely hear you. I'm walking through traffic."

Marianne laughed, her heart soaring. "Well, you won't find that kind of noise and traffic out here at the beach. Just peace and serenity."

There was a pause. "Oh my gosh, is this Ms. Mueller?"

"Marianne. Yes."

"I just sent my resume from the Starbucks on the corner. Like twenty minutes ago."

"Perfect timing! I'd love to meet you."

"Really?" The happiness in the woman's voice radiated through the connection.

"Yes, really."

"For an audition?"

Marianne hesitated. Was an audition even necessary? This woman had a resume a mile long. If all those qualified directors in the Big Apple had auditioned and selected her, who was she to turn her down? She looked the part, and Marianne's show needed its Marian.

"Let me ask you this, do you know any of the music from *The Music Man*?"

got her luggage, piled into the car and drove the
 distance to Pawleys, Stella doing her fair share of
 and Marianne trying to get to know her star as best
 ld in Stella's gaps. When they reached the bridge that
 oss to the island, Roxanne moaned. "Oh my, it's so
 l. I mean, look at it!"

anne smiled. Despite growing up and living her whole
 the island, she tried to never take for granted the
 of her surroundings. "Are you a beach fan?"

anne looked embarrassed. "Believe it or not, I haven't
 d much. I can't honestly say I've done much beach
 grew up in Ohio, and I moved to New York. That's

w," Marianne murmured. She couldn't imagine a life
 the ocean and sand and sunsets. "You'll have plenty
 to explore and become a beach lover."

en they arrived at the Inn, Stella and Marianne helped
 e carry her bags in. Marianne told her daughter,
 be in Room 10, Stella."

ay!" she replied excitedly. She loved helping, and she
 e way importantly to the upstairs guest rooms.
 ne handed her the key and she unlocked the #10
 wung it open and stepped back.

anne winked at Stella and stepped past her, into the
 Marianne watched her examine the room and tried to
 as Roxanne would. The bleached wood floors and
 g, paired with the oceanfront window, caused the sun
 e in and bathe the whole room with warmth and light.
 o double beds with matching peach and mint-colored
 s. The rocking chair in the corner with the small table
 an invitation to come and read or rest. Two doors led

"What, are you kidding? Of course I do. It's one of my favorite musicals of all time."

Marianne chuckled. "Sing me something."

"What, right now?"

"Yep."

It only took Roxanne five seconds to launch into "Till There Was You," the sentimental love song between Marian and Harold. And it only took Marianne five seconds to know, without a doubt, that she had found her Marian. The rest of the song, she just closed her eyes and savored it.

When she finished, Marianne heard what she assumed was a taxi horn. "That was beautiful. Thank you."

"You're welcome."

"Have you played Marian before?"

"No, but it's always been a dream role of mine. Another reason why I'm so interested in your production."

"You say New York's starting to get to you?"

The woman sighed. "You could say that. I'm not from here originally. I'm here following my dream. It's … hard. I need a break. But I want to keep performing."

"Roxanne … you may think I'm crazy but … will you come to Pawleys Island and play Marian?"

She screamed. "That's it? I'm hired?"

Marianne laughed. "You're perfect. And I need you. You saw the terms listed on my posting. You have any problems with those?"

"Hmmm, let's see. Free room and board in a vacation resort. Performing two, three nights a week, and the rest of the week to sunbathe and sightsee. And a little pocket money to boot? No. I don't have a problem with that."

They discussed logistics — Marianne would email her the abridged script and Roxanne would begin memorizing it immediately. Marianne would book her a one-way airline ticket just as soon as she could get one, and send her the arrangements.

"Oh, one other thing," Marianne said. "Do you happen to know a Harold?"

Chapter Fift[een]

It only took four days to get Roxann[e ...] packed Stella in the car and drove [to the] Airport to pick her up. Stella spott[ed ... as she] walked into sight, due to Marian[ne ...] headshot with her. In Stella's mind, [... was a] celebrity and this was the most exciti[ng thing that had] happened in her five years. Her little [... of] arriving Marian Paroo bordered on obs[ession.]

Marianne handed her daughter th[e sign she had] finished creating less than an h[our before.] "ROXANNE" surrounded by colorf[ul ...] Stella held it high above her head, and [... success] in locating them, she jumped up and d[own ...]

Roxanne laughed and waved. She [... and] Stella said excitedly, "Hi Roxanne!"

Roxanne squatted so she was mor[e ... "]Thanks for coming to pick me up."

Marianne held her hand out and [... "I'm] Marianne and this is my daughter, S[tella. We're so] excited to have you here."

"And I couldn't be more excited to [be here. The] temperature rose at least twenty five de[grees ...] to here, and I'm assuming I won't see a[ny ... or] any smog."

to a small bath, and a tiny closet. It was the essence of modest coziness.

The New York resident turned in a circle, her eyes lit up with excitement. If Marianne had a split second of worry that it wasn't up to standard, she relaxed quickly. Roxanne appeared to love it.

"It's perfect. Can I just say thank you very much for picking me for this job? It's *so* what the doctor ordered right now, I can't even tell you what a needed break this is. I'm so thankful for this opportunity, I'm going to work my butt off to be the absolute best Marian you've ever seen!" She covered the steps between them and pulled Marianne into an embrace so genuine, Marianne breathed a word of thanks to God for leading her to this girl.

They chatted a moment about the room, and then Marianne dragged a beaming Stella out of the room. "You've had a busy day of travel, and you've got several hours now to rest, to get settled in, to check out the beach, whatever. Just so you know, you're welcome in the dining room for three meals a day, 8:30, 1:15 and 6:15. Rehearsals are at 7:30. We'll be fitting your costumes over the next few days, and we're shooting for Opening Night in a little over a week. Any questions whatsoever, please just let me know. I'm always around. Tonight I'll introduce you to the directors and the rest of the cast."

Roxanne smiled. "I think I'm going to love it here."

"We're so glad you joined us."

Marianne was floating high all day with the addition of Roxanne to the cast. She invited Leslie to have dinner at the Inn before rehearsal, so she, Leslie and Roxanne could get to know each other over the meal. When the three of them gathered in the dining room, Marianne put one hand on Leslie's arm and one on Roxanne's.

"Leslie, this is Roxanne. She's joining the cast today as Marian!"

Leslie beamed a smile at Roxanne and grasped her hand. "So happy to have you, Roxanne. You look perfect for Marian."

Roxanne laughed. "Well, thank you very much. I love this play and I've always wanted to play Marian, so this is a dream come true for me."

"What musicals have you been in before?" Leslie asked and Marianne slid a copy of Roxanne's resume over toward her plate. Leslie picked it up and studied it. "Oh my goodness. You have some great experience. And I see you're joining us from an off-Broadway show in New York? However did we get so lucky to secure you? I know Marianne can be persuasive, but how exactly did she pull this off?"

Roxanne's smile mellowed. "Have you ever just felt like going off the beaten path? Like the way your life is headed may have been exactly what you planned for yourself, but once you got there you realized it's not what you wanted?"

Leslie's mouth dropped and she gazed over at Marianne, then back to Roxanne. "Oh, you have no idea." The two of them laughed. "In answer, yes, I have felt exactly that way, and followed my whim and ended up with my life taking a completely opposite turn. And I've never been happier."

Roxanne nodded. "I needed a change. Quickly. And this job posting just spoke to me. In fact, it grabbed me and wouldn't let go. So I sent an email, and figured, if it's meant to be, it'll be. Twenty minutes later, I get a phone call with a job offer. And here I am."

Leslie patted her hand. "Do you believe in God, dear?"

"What, are you kidding? Of course I do. It's one of my favorite musicals of all time."

Marianne chuckled. "Sing me something."

"What, right now?"

"Yep."

It only took Roxanne five seconds to launch into "Till There Was You," the sentimental love song between Marian and Harold. And it only took Marianne five seconds to know, without a doubt, that she had found her Marian. The rest of the song, she just closed her eyes and savored it.

When she finished, Marianne heard what she assumed was a taxi horn. "That was beautiful. Thank you."

"You're welcome."

"Have you played Marian before?"

"No, but it's always been a dream role of mine. Another reason why I'm so interested in your production."

"You say New York's starting to get to you?"

The woman sighed. "You could say that. I'm not from here originally. I'm here following my dream. It's ... hard. I need a break. But I want to keep performing."

"Roxanne ... you may think I'm crazy but ... will you come to Pawleys Island and play Marian?"

She screamed. "That's it? I'm hired?"

Marianne laughed. "You're perfect. And I need you. You saw the terms listed on my posting. You have any problems with those?"

"Hmmm, let's see. Free room and board in a vacation resort. Performing two, three nights a week, and the rest of the week to sunbathe and sightsee. And a little pocket money to boot? No. I don't have a problem with that."

They discussed logistics — Marianne would email her the abridged script and Roxanne would begin memorizing it immediately. Marianne would book her a one-way airline ticket just as soon as she could get one, and send her the arrangements.

"Oh, one other thing," Marianne said. "Do you happen to know a Harold?"

Chapter Fifteen

It only took four days to get Roxanne to Pawleys. Marianne packed Stella in the car and drove to the Myrtle Beach Airport to pick her up. Stella spotted her the minute she walked into sight, due to Marianne sharing Roxanne's headshot with her. In Stella's mind, Roxanne was a huge celebrity and this was the most exciting thing that had ever happened in her five years. Her little girl adulation of their arriving Marian Paroo bordered on obsessive.

Marianne handed her daughter the sign that Stella had finished creating less than an hour ago, the name "ROXANNE" surrounded by colorful flowers and birds. Stella held it high above her head, and to further aid Roxanne in locating them, she jumped up and down in place as well.

Roxanne laughed and waved. She approached them and Stella said excitedly, "Hi Roxanne!"

Roxanne squatted so she was more Stella's height. "Hi! Thanks for coming to pick me up."

Marianne held her hand out and helped her up. "I'm Marianne and this is my daughter, Stella. We're both so excited to have you here."

"And I couldn't be more excited to be here. I believe the temperature rose at least twenty five degrees from New York to here, and I'm assuming I won't see a traffic jam or breathe any smog."

They got her luggage, piled into the car and drove the short distance to Pawleys, Stella doing her fair share of chatter and Marianne trying to get to know her star as best she could in Stella's gaps. When they reached the bridge that led across to the island, Roxanne moaned. "Oh my, it's so beautiful. I mean, look at it!"

Marianne smiled. Despite growing up and living her whole life on the island, she tried to never take for granted the beauty of her surroundings. "Are you a beach fan?"

Roxanne looked embarrassed. "Believe it or not, I haven't travelled much. I can't honestly say I've done much beach time. I grew up in Ohio, and I moved to New York. That's it."

"Wow," Marianne murmured. She couldn't imagine a life without the ocean and sand and sunsets. "You'll have plenty of time to explore and become a beach lover."

When they arrived at the Inn, Stella and Marianne helped Roxanne carry her bags in. Marianne told her daughter, "She'll be in Room 10, Stella."

"Okay!" she replied excitedly. She loved helping, and she led the way importantly to the upstairs guest rooms. Marianne handed her the key and she unlocked the #10 door, swung it open and stepped back.

Roxanne winked at Stella and stepped past her, into the room. Marianne watched her examine the room and tried to see it as Roxanne would. The bleached wood floors and paneling, paired with the oceanfront window, caused the sun to come in and bathe the whole room with warmth and light. The two double beds with matching peach and mint-colored spreads. The rocking chair in the corner with the small table beside, an invitation to come and read or rest. Two doors led to a small bath, and a tiny closet. It was the essence of modest coziness.

The New York resident turned in a circle, her eyes lit up with excitement. If Marianne had a split second of worry that it wasn't up to standard, she relaxed quickly. Roxanne appeared to love it.

"It's perfect. Can I just say thank you very much for picking me for this job? It's *so* what the doctor ordered right now, I can't even tell you what a needed break this is. I'm so thankful for this opportunity, I'm going to work my butt off to be the absolute best Marian you've ever seen!" She covered the steps between them and pulled Marianne into an embrace so genuine, Marianne breathed a word of thanks to God for leading her to this girl.

They chatted a moment about the room, and then Marianne dragged a beaming Stella out of the room. "You've had a busy day of travel, and you've got several hours now to rest, to get settled in, to check out the beach, whatever. Just so you know, you're welcome in the dining room for three meals a day, 8:30, 1:15 and 6:15. Rehearsals are at 7:30. We'll be fitting your costumes over the next few days, and we're shooting for Opening Night in a little over a week. Any questions whatsoever, please just let me know. I'm always around. Tonight I'll introduce you to the directors and the rest of the cast."

Roxanne smiled. "I think I'm going to love it here."

"We're so glad you joined us."

Marianne was floating high all day with the addition of Roxanne to the cast. She invited Leslie to have dinner at the Inn before rehearsal, so she, Leslie and Roxanne could get to know each other over the meal. When the three of them gathered in the dining room, Marianne put one hand on Leslie's arm and one on Roxanne's.

"Leslie, this is Roxanne. She's joining the cast today as Marian!"

Leslie beamed a smile at Roxanne and grasped her hand. "So happy to have you, Roxanne. You look perfect for Marian."

Roxanne laughed. "Well, thank you very much. I love this play and I've always wanted to play Marian, so this is a dream come true for me."

"What musicals have you been in before?" Leslie asked and Marianne slid a copy of Roxanne's resume over toward her plate. Leslie picked it up and studied it. "Oh my goodness. You have some great experience. And I see you're joining us from an off-Broadway show in New York? However did we get so lucky to secure you? I know Marianne can be persuasive, but how exactly did she pull this off?"

Roxanne's smile mellowed. "Have you ever just felt like going off the beaten path? Like the way your life is headed may have been exactly what you planned for yourself, but once you got there you realized it's not what you wanted?"

Leslie's mouth dropped and she gazed over at Marianne, then back to Roxanne. "Oh, you have no idea." The two of them laughed. "In answer, yes, I have felt exactly that way, and followed my whim and ended up with my life taking a completely opposite turn. And I've never been happier."

Roxanne nodded. "I needed a change. Quickly. And this job posting just spoke to me. In fact, it grabbed me and wouldn't let go. So I sent an email, and figured, if it's meant to be, it'll be. Twenty minutes later, I get a phone call with a job offer. And here I am."

Leslie patted her hand. "Do you believe in God, dear?"

Roxanne shrugged. "Not really. I mean, I don't *not* believe. But I'm not a staunch believer, if you know what I mean."

Leslie held a hand up. "Not a problem. It just sounded an awful lot like God's hand directing your life. Something I've had a lot of experience with. Regardless, we're happy you're here."

They all enjoyed a low country dinner of Jambalaya over red rice, a fresh green salad and cornbread. They shared stories and by the end of the meal, the conversation came back to the dinner theater.

"If you serve food like this along with the performance, you'll have lines out the door and we'll have to increase to five shows a week," Roxanne said.

"I'm lucky to have one of the best chefs in town, and he makes at least ten meals a week — all this good. He's responsible for all dinners, and half the lunches. I have a second chef responsible for breakfasts and half the lunches. I can attest to the food's tastiness. I've gained twelve pounds since I hired them."

"I'll have to be careful then, so I don't have to let out my costumes."

"Daily walks on the beach help out with burning calories," Leslie said.

Marianne pulled her notebook, never far from her, over. "All my details are coming together. Ticket sales are good. We're sold out for the first weekend, rehearsals are on schedule, costumes are here, just need to be fitted. And we have our Marian! Roxanne, how many rehearsals do you think you'll need your script?"

"None. I memorized it all."

Marianne gestured a "whew" to Leslie, who said, "Hey, she's a pro."

"There's just one big fat hole. And it's Harold. We haven't cast Harold yet, and he's such an important part. Obviously. He's the title role. He *is* the Music Man. We can't proceed without him." She placed a pleading glance on Roxanne. "Do you know of anyone in New York you could convince to come? Even if they can't commit to the whole run, just for the first few weekends? Anyone at all from your musical theater connections?"

The girl looked like she was on the verge of giving a name, and Marianne was poised to write it down, along with a phone number so she could pursue him and put her persuasiveness to the test. But Roxanne pulled back. "No one I can think of at the moment, who is available. Or willing to leave the city." She rushed on when she saw Marianne's disappointment, "But I'll keep brainstorming. I used to have an agent. I could call him and float it by him as well."

"Oh thank you, whatever you can do."

As Marianne and Leslie expected, Roxanne was a hit with the children, the adult cast and the full staff of directors and musicians. She was a natural, and lent such a breath of fresh air. She knew her lines, learned her staging quickly, and had all the songs down to a tee.

A few nights later, the cast had all received their costumes. Alterations were underway and Leslie and the music director were double and triple checking the songs that featured Marian with the townspeople or family members. Roxanne stood on stage with the little boy playing Winthrop and the woman playing her mother. They were rehearsing the crowd favorite, "Gary, Indiana." Winthrop had perfected his lisp and was using it to full comedic effect. Marianne knew once the room was full of appreciative theatergoers, the song would elicit lots of laughter and applause.

She sat in the dining room, observing the rehearsal and checking her laptop every thirty seconds for some sort of reaction to her posting for a Harold. Her mind half on the song, and half on her email, she was suddenly confused when Roxanne came to a halt right before singing, "Gary," and instead yelled, "Tieg!" Marianne jerked her head up.

A tall, handsome man stood in the center of the dining room facing the stage. He stared at Roxanne, his mouth open wide in pleasure, a hint of a smile forming on his lips. "Roxanne."

Marianne let her eyes follow his. But Roxanne's face didn't mirror his obvious pleasure. Hers looked concerned, her eyebrows diving, lines of concern etched in her brow. Marianne got to her feet and as she approached the stage, the piano accompanist stopped playing and even Winthrop's solo filtered off. Suddenly the room was silent, waiting to see what would happen next.

"I found you!" the man said.

Marianne climbed up on the stage and took Roxanne's arm, guided her off to the side. "Roxanne, do you know this man?"

She nodded, her eyes darting in all directions. "Yes, yes I do. Tieg Miller. My ... my ...," she turned and looked at him again and turned back. "My acting partner."

"Your ...? Oh! He's an actor?" Marianne's heart jumped into her throat. Roxanne had spread the word to her actor friends. She had her Harold Hill! She turned and motioned Leslie over, then turned again and motioned to Tieg as well. They both climbed up and joined them, a foursome huddled onstage.

"So, Tieg, I'm Marianne Mueller, I'm the producer of the show. This is Leslie Harrison, she's the director. And of course, you know Roxanne. She's playing Marian. But of course, you know that." She turned to Roxanne. "Did you recruit him? Does he know the part?"

Roxanne was unusually quiet and didn't respond.

"Roxanne? What's going on? Do I have this wrong?" Marianne asked.

"Yes," Roxanne responded, just as Tieg said, "No." They looked at each other, Roxanne's a glare at her acting partner.

"I'd like the part," Tieg said and then grunted in pain. A movement caused Marianne to glance at the floor, where Roxanne had stomped on his foot.

"I'm confused," Marianne said. "We need a Professor Harold Hill desperately or we can't do the show. I've tried everything. I've listed the show on several actor websites, I've placed casting call ads in industry magazines and I've searched headshot sites. No takers. I've about lost hope. And the show is absolutely wonderful, except we don't have a Harold."

Tieg furrowed his brow, then leaned close to Marianne. "*The Music Man*, right?"

"Yes."

"Right, right!" he said with glee. Roxanne gave him an irritated expression. "I can do it. I'd be happy to do it."

"That's good to hear. But could you wait just a moment? I need a word with Leslie and Roxanne."

He nodded and backed up, reaching the end of the stage without taking his eyes off Roxanne.

Marianne watched him, then turned to her leading lady. "So, what's going on? You could cut the tension between you two with a knife. I assumed you'd talked to him about the role, and he showed up without telling you. But now I'm picking up that you really don't want him here."

Roxanne sputtered, went silent, opened her mouth again. Then she sighed. "I don't want to get into it. Yes, we have some history. He was one of the reasons I needed a break from New York. Although I can't *believe* he followed me to Pawleys Island, … I can *so* see him following me to Pawleys Island."

Leslie gasped. "Is he abusive?"

Roxanne's eyes popped wider. "Abusive? What, you mean like physically? No, no, no. We aren't together. He's not my boyfriend, and no, he's never abused me." She turned to Marianne, then back to Leslie. "He just annoys me. And him being here puts a real damper on my carefree sabbatical to the beach, I don't mind telling you."

Marianne felt like crying. She had no idea if this Tieg fellow even had the talent to play the part, but he was her best candidate yet. Okay, her *only* candidate yet. But she wanted Roxanne to be happy. She'd gotten Roxanne first, and she felt some loyalty to her.

She turned to the actress. "We'll just ask him to leave. I want you to be happy and comfortable and able to perform your best. Obviously, he stresses you out. For whatever reason."

Roxanne gazed down at her feet, thinking. She looked back at Marianne and Leslie. "But I can't perform my best without a leading man, can I? Tieg is good, and we have chemistry because we've worked together before."

"Does he have a resume like yours?" Marianne dared to ask, almost hoping the answer was no.

"Longer. He's been a New York actor for seven years, supporting himself on his performances. He's got a voice like you wouldn't believe."

Marianne smiled. "Sounds like you're trying to convince me to hire him."

Roxanne rolled her eyes. "He grows on you. How about this? You keep looking for a replacement. But we can use him in the meantime."

It was the best solution she could possibly hope for. She pulled Roxanne into a hug and the girl chuckled in her ear. "Are you sure?"

"Yeah, I guess. I'll just have to lay the groundwork with him, that's all. We'll be fine."

When they broke apart, Marianne glanced over at Tieg. He was studying all their movements, a hopeful expression on his face. She motioned to him and he trotted over.

"Tieg, we're going to cast you in the role of Professor Harold Hill."

He pumped a fist into the air.

"But … I'm going to continue to look for another actor. Roxanne didn't tell us what has happened between you two, but she's not entirely happy that you showed up here after she'd taken the job. We'll see how it goes the first few weekends of performance, and see if I have to replace you."

He rested a pointed gaze on Roxanne, who remained expressionless, then he turned back to Marianne. "Sounds fair."

"Rehearsals start at 7:30 tonight. I'll walk you to your room and cover the terms of the employment contract."

"Okay."

Marianne wasn't sure what their history was all about, but she was sure of several things: the man was attractive, she could definitely see him in the role of a con man convincing an entire town that he was someone he was not, and … she finally had her complete cast.

Full steam ahead.

* * *

Tieg delivered. His singing voice sent chills down everyone's spines and his demeanor onstage was perfect for the role. Even while holding a paper copy of the script, Marianne and Leslie could tell he embodied the part. Despite how difficult it was to entice two experienced, professional actors to leave New York and come to Pawleys Island to do a small dinner theater, they ended up with the two perfect actors for their show. When theater is done well, and the actors are talented, they have chemistry with each other, and the music they perform is on track and sing-alongable, magic happens in the hearts of the audience members. This production appeared to have magic that not even Marianne and Leslie could've dreamed of.

Because he was a pro, by the third rehearsal, Tieg had his extensive part completely committed to memory. Because he had worked with Roxanne so many times before, they fit each other like a glove. And because the supporting cast had worked on their songs and parts for weeks prior to the leads being cast, they all knew what they were doing. The Opening Night date that Marianne had randomly picked to list on her dinner theater website appeared to be do-able.

Now, that date was only a few days away. Emma came up with the idea of inviting as many regional journalists as possible to a Dress Rehearsal preview night. With Emma's hard work and contacts, they ended up with twenty publications represented, magazines, newspapers and online news blogs.

The night following, Emma organized a "Pay What You Can" night for community members who couldn't afford the full dinner theater price. So, a nearly full house of eighty five grateful people came just for the show, not the dinner, some paying five dollars, some paying as much as twenty. Considering it was a Dress Rehearsal anyway, that wouldn't have normally drawn any earnings at all, and considering it created a buzz around town to get people interested in attending, Marianne considered it a huge success.

Emma was proving to be worth her weight in gold from a marketing perspective.

The morning of Opening Night, Marianne awoke with a combination of excitement and nervousness. She gazed over at Tom, still sleeping. A wash of disappointment flooded her. Although they were sharing a bed, their relationship had crumbled to the point that they shared little else. She'd returned to their shared bed after one night away because she didn't want to worry Stella. Surely, being as bright a girl as she was, she'd notice if either of them moved out of their little apartment permanently. However, if Stella would wander into their bedroom while they were sleeping, she would surely notice the Great Divide between their two bodies on the mattress. It seemed important to Tom as well as herself, to have no unnecessary touching of limbs during this endless conflict.

She was still furious at him for his stance on Jeremy, so she rarely had a conversation with him. She was keeping busy with the dinner theater, and he was busy single-handedly running the daily operations of the Inn. They rarely crossed paths. She missed him. She missed their closeness and their intimacy.

But the way things stood, she couldn't imagine a way to dig out of the rut they were in, and return to a true, loving marriage.

As she stared at him, he opened his eyes. When he saw her, he smiled. She turned her head, afraid that her eyes would reflect her feelings.

"Big day, honey."

She nodded.

"You've worked hard, and I admire you very much. It looks like you've really pulled this off. I've seen enough of the dress rehearsals to see that you've got a quality show there."

She rose from bed and went to her mirror. "Well, I've had a lot of help. I didn't do it alone." Despite that fact that he hadn't given her any help whatsoever. She shook her head, trying to shake away the negative thoughts.

"What can I do to help you tonight? I've got two new guests checking in by six tonight, but I want to be available to help out with Opening Night."

She blinked, considering. Although she thought she had all the bases covered, it would be nice to have another set of eyes on the evening. "Could you help Toby and his assistants in the kitchen? They're accustomed to producing around forty meals at a time for our regular guests, but he's never had to produce a hundred, all being served within minutes of each other."

"You want me to serve?"

"No, not serve. The performers are all assigned to wait on a table or two, which helps them earn tips from their tables.

But you could help out in the kitchen, preparing the plates, or just doing what Toby tells you."

"Sure, honey."

"And during the show, just hang backstage and keep an eye out for anything that goes wrong. I'll be out front viewing the stage and helping out wherever needed. You know, just a floater to take care of unexpected problems."

He smiled. "I can do that." He rose out of bed and joined her. He put a hand on her shoulder and laid his face in her hair. Marianne tightened, but forced herself not to move. "I'm sorry things are so strained between us. Especially on such an important night for our business. I want us to work together on this."

She couldn't stop a roll of the eyes. Work together? When, now? When all the work has been done and all that's left is the glory? Now, he wants to work together?

She could've said a hundred words in response. She could've said that things didn't have to be so strained. That all he'd have to do was to forgive Jeremy for his past errors, to accept her brother as a full member of their extended family, and to be happy for him in his pending marriage to Emma. But Tom knew how she felt. They had discussed it ad nauseum, and she wasn't about it get into it now. Opening Night deserved her full attention today.

So she said, "We'll see," and she moved into the shower.

* * *

Marianne spent the day hitting Refresh on her laptop and marveling over how many tickets to their production they'd sold. Not only was Opening Night completely sold out, but the next few performances were sold out as well. Emma's marketing strategies were evidently working.

Around five, Marianne started to panic that something would go wrong. That the food for Toby's opening dinner would be spoiled, and harbored some parasite that would cause all their guests to go running for the bathroom halfway through the second act. Then she imagined all the children in the cast forgetting their songs and their training, inflicted with stage fright when the lights shone on them. Then she worried that Roxanne and Tieg would let their past history, whatever it contained, get to them and they'd no longer be able to work together. Actors could be emotional — what if they had a fight and refused to go on as long as the other one was there?

But soon, all her fears were proven to be unfounded. The Inn filled with the aroma of fresh-baked bread and a delicious surf and turf combination — fried shrimp and filet mignon. The actors started arriving and getting into costume. Her dad came and did a technical check on the lights and the mikes. Leslie went through last minute pointers with the kids, and the music director warmed up the small orchestra.

The entire Inn looked, sounded and smelled like a dinner theater.

The guests started arriving. Marianne manned the Box Office. "Thank you for coming to our Opening Night," she told one older couple.

The woman smiled. "It's one of my favorite musicals, and you can't beat free tickets. Great idea, by the way, partnering with local businesses."

Marianne, confused, focused on printing out the tickets and handing them to her. "I'm sorry, what?"

The woman took the tickets and waved them at her. "Didn't you partner with Harrison Designs at the Grand Opening of their furniture store? They had a whole promotion, depending on how much you spent there, how many free tickets they'd give you. We bought a whole bedroom set and received four free tickets. My husband and I are here tonight, and my daughter and her husband are coming tomorrow night."

Marianne stared at her, her mind racing. Jeremy? He'd never even mentioned this to her. But the next customer in line stepped up and she had to push it out of her mind.

For Marianne, the evening was a fleeting stream of snippets.

"This is the best shrimp I've ever had. You must provide the recipe."

Anticipation building as the orchestra opened the show with a medley of Music Man songs.

The opening act, the train ride, lyrics spoken in *chug-chug-chug* rhythm, performed to perfection by Tieg and the men of the cast.

The soaring voices of Roxanne and Tieg, singing in duet.

The children, dressed in period clothing, remembering their songs and their staging, smiling adorably.

Lights on, lights off.

Applause, applause and more applause.

Desserts being delivered to each table during intermission by busy actors.

Smiles and laughter and more applause.

Before she knew it, it was over, the cast all stuffed up onstage together, holding hands, bowing, and then Leslie, soaking up applause, calling Marianne's name through the microphone. She was in such a daze, she barely made her way around the crowded tables, people patting her as she passed them. She must have made it up the stairs, onto the stage, into the bosom of the company. A whoop of appreciation rose up from the actors behind her, simultaneously with the audience in front of her.

Then, it was over. Silence, ears ringing, recovering from the mound of noise, now gone. Time to do it all again tomorrow night.

She popped open bottles of champagne for the adult cast members, soda bottles for the kids. They all rose their glasses in a toast for the success of their show. She said a silent prayer to God, a thank you for believing in her and helping her in pulling this off, every step of the way.

Everyone had had a great time, and couldn't wait for tomorrow. The cast members all filtered out. Leslie and her dad stayed till the very end, telling her how proud they were of her. She couldn't have done it without both of them, and she told them so.

Quiet again, she made sure everything was secured and ready for the night, and wandered back toward their apartment. Tom stood behind the guest desk. He looked up. "What a night. You're not going to believe how much money we brought in." He jotted down a number on a slip of paper, drew two lines underneath it and slid it over to her. "If we make this every night, then I have no idea why we never tried this before. I bow to your much better judgment."

She shook her head, laughed, and kept walking. It had started out about the money, but it was about so much more than that now. The dinner theater was life-changing for her, as well as everyone who'd worked on it, both on and behind the stage. Leave it to Tom to only look at the monetary gains of the evening.

Chapter Sixteen

Mid-week, Marianne received a text message from Jeremy: "If you have a sec, stop by the store."

Marianne grinned. Of course she had a "sec" for her big brother. She left immediately and got in the car. When she arrived at the store she was happy to see Jeremy working with a customer, pointing out various wooden pieces. He lifted his head when she walked in, smiled and held up a finger to her. She made herself busy walking around, examining all the beautiful pieces he'd built.

About twenty minutes later, he wrapped up the sale, said good-bye to his customers and walked over to her. "Sorry about that. When I sent you the text, I had no idea you'd come right over."

She gave him a mischievous glare. "So, how many free dinner theater tickets did that sale result in? Or was that promotion only for your Grand Opening?"

He opened his mouth, closed it, and ducked his head. "Oh."

She punched him on the arm. "What were you thinking?"

"Marianne, I've always told you that somehow, someday, I would repay you for all the generosity you've shown me over the past nine months. The free room, the free meals, the advertising ideas, the storage space. Emma and I decided this might be a nice idea. So, we offered tickets to your show to our most generous customers. Seemed like a win/win."

Marianne giggled, her happiness and appreciation bubbling out of her. "The first three shows were absolutely awesome. Great performances, full houses. I couldn't be more pleased."

He nodded. "So I've heard."

She looked at him. "From who?"

"Well, for one, I've gotten phone calls and emails from at least a half dozen customers who received free tickets. They enjoyed it so much, they're all going back. And giving gifts of tickets to their friends and relatives."

"Wow."

"And for another, have you read the newspapers? The reviews are out the roof."

"Thanks to your fiancé. Her idea to offer a press preview night was genius."

He nodded, his grin remaining.

"You know, this show has some staying power. But even if it ended after next weekend, it will have been worth it."

"Dream big, sis. I can see this becoming a regular part of your Inn. I could see Seaside Inn becoming known for not only its great beach, quaint rooms and awesome food, but the best dinner theater productions in the region."

She stepped into his arms for a warm hug. She was glad she came over, her heart was so full of love and happiness.

"So," Jeremy said, "in addition to congratulating you on your success, I had another reason to invite you over." He looked around and found a nearby bar stool, and offered her a seat, sitting himself.

"Yes?"

He gripped his hands together, then rubbed them on his thighs. "You know how I gave Emma a ring?"

A grin burst out on her face. "Yes, a beautiful ruby."

"Well, I thought it was just an indication that I loved her. I thought I'd take my time to build my business, to save some money, and someday, I'd propose to her."

"I hear a but coming on."

He nodded. "But ... someday is now."

Marianne gasped.

"Emma saw no reason to wait. She convinced me that we love each other, and waiting a few years wouldn't accomplish anything. She loves the ring, and considers it her engagement ring. She doesn't want a second one with a diamond in it. So, once a couple is engaged, what comes next?"

"They get married!"

"Yes. So ..."

"You're getting married?"

"Yes. We are. Soon. We're having a very short engagement. We want to be together, so we're going to make it happen."

"Oh, Jeremy." She jumped off her stool and nearly knocked him off his, plowing into him with a over-enthusiastic embrace. "I'm so happy for you. I really am." She hopped back on her stool. "Tell me all the arrangements."

"Okay. A little non-traditional. We didn't want to intrude on any dinner theater performances, so we're doing it on a weeknight. Two Wednesday nights from now, in fact. We'll have the ceremony at the church Emma and I have been attending together. We'll have a reception, if you want to call it that, more like a small social gathering afterward at Dad and Leslie's."

"How perfect! The Old Grey Barn has a proud history of hosting successful weddings."

He nodded. Just last fall, their dad surprised his bride Leslie with a wedding in their dream home on their move-in day. It was a magical day, and the start to a very happy marriage.

"Emma's made out a guest list. It'll be small. Her friends from school, from work, our fellow church members. And my family members."

Of course, Emma had a lot of friends but few family members. And Jeremy had a lot of family members, but few friends. They were a perfect complement.

"What will you wear?"

"Despite the impromptu nature of the wedding, and the small size, Emma wants us to go traditional with the clothes. She's picked out a white dress — not floor length, but still formal. And I'm renting a tux, at her request."

"Oh, you'll look so handsome."

He shook his head.

"Do you need a flower girl?"

He went silent, staring at her for a moment. "Are you referring to Stella?"

She scoffed. "Of course I'm referring to Stella."

He looked to the floor. "I've already had this discussion with Emma. She wanted to ask Stella as well. In fact, she already bought her a little dress that matches the bridesmaids'. But I don't think it's a good idea."

Marianne frowned. She didn't even have to ask why. Of course, Jeremy, being the honorable guy he was, didn't want to go against Tom's ultimatum. Regardless of how ridiculous it was.

"It's a special, once-in-a-lifetime occasion. One that Stella would be heartbroken to miss."

Jeremy shook his head. "I have to honor Tom's wishes here, sis. What you do is up to you. But Tom doesn't want Stella to be around me and Emma. So the last thing I want to do is to dishonor Tom by having her in our wedding."

"But Jeremy, Tom is wrong."

"You think he is. And I think he is. But in his mind, he's doing the right thing. He's doing it out of love and protection for Stella. So, I have to honor that."

Marianne's heart deflated like a balloon losing air. She'd been so happy to hear the news, and now this. "Am I invited to your wedding?"

"You're both invited, you and Tom. But I'll leave it up to you whether you come or not."

She laid a hand on his arm. "An army couldn't keep me away."

* * *

On Friday, Tom prepared for his parents' arrival. He had called them after the debut weekend of the dinner theater, ecstatic over the successful production. They were so excited, they made plans to attend. They would arrive in the afternoon, attend the dinner show, spend the night and enjoy a little beach time the next day, then head home.

Since he and Marianne hadn't been communicating up to their normal standard, he sought her out as she bustled around the stage with her notebook, following notes she'd taken the previous weekend, direction on what to change about the sets. "Marianne? Could I take a few minutes of your time?"

She nodded, held a finger up, and finished nudging a potted plant what looked like a half inch to the left of where it was before. She came to the foot of the stage where he stood on the floor. With the chilliness between them lately since Jeremy and Emma's engagement and now pending wedding, he told himself to feel lucky that he'd gotten that.

"Sweetheart," he started, "my parents are visiting. I told them how successful the production was, and they want to see it themselves. They'll arrive in the next few hours, and leave tomorrow."

She took the news with what looked like a genuine smile. Of course, why wouldn't it be genuine? Marianne had always loved his parents, and they adored her. It wasn't them she was angry at — he alone deserved that honor.

"Great! What room are you putting them in?"

"Number 12."

"Good, I was hoping that one was vacant." It was one of their larger rooms, with newer linens and bedspread. "Too bad they can't stay longer."

"Yeah, Dad has ... something."

Marianne chuckled and his heart overflowed unexpectedly with love for her. She was such a part of him. She'd been there for him for the most important events of his life — falling in love, committing himself to another, marriage, childbirth, starting a business. His family loved her almost as much as he did. He couldn't even eke out an image of his life without her. Their feud had gone on way too long, and was throwing him off. But he couldn't just give in because he knew she didn't like his stance. Just like he knew she couldn't give in to him for the same reason.

"Figures. That man sure keeps busy, doesn't he?"

Tom smiled. "Stella will be so excited to perform for them tonight."

"She sure will. I assume you'll take care of their check-in and I'll see them eventually." She waved a hand and returned to study the flaws in the set.

When they arrived, there was the usual loud Mueller raised-voice greetings, hugs, back pats and smiles. His mother was the extrovert of the couple, and his dad the doting introvert. In his parents' case, "opposites attract" was a way of life. His mother was a sweetheart, but you couldn't get a word in edgewise around her. He helped them bring in their bags, and listened to Mom ooze compliments about the room, the view, the ocean and the Inn. They discussed *The Music Man*, what a great idea it was of Marianne's to produce it, and they couldn't wait to see it.

Of course they discussed Stella and her scary episode, and their thankfulness that the counselor had given her a complete release from further sessions.

An hour into the visit, Tom asked his dad if he could steal him away for some father/son time. His mother was thrilled at the request, and vowed to stay busy unpacking and resting. Tom led his dad downstairs, out the back porch and onto the sand.

"Want to leave our shoes here and walk barefoot?" Tom asked.

His dad was game. The first ten minutes, they walked in silence, which Tom knew was just fine with his dad. But the man was wise, and Tom really needed his counsel. So he chose his words carefully.

"Dad, I don't want to go into a lot of personal details, but I need your advice. Marital advice. Marianne and I have hit a bit of an icy patch, and it's not getting any better. Darned if I'm not at a loss for what to do next."

His dad looked over at him as they walked. "I'm sorry to hear that, son."

"Do you and Mom ever fight?"

The older man broke out with a laugh. "Of course. All married people fight with each other."

Tom glanced over at his dad. "Really? I don't remember you guys fighting much at all."

"We made it a point not to fight in front of you kids. But sure, we had disagreements. We didn't agree with each other on everything. We're such completely different people, it was inevitable."

"Huh. I had no idea."

He and Marianne really hadn't fought much, if at all, prior to Jeremy being released from prison. In fact, everything they'd ever disagreed about had centered around Jeremy. Knowing that his parents had disagreements regularly when he was a child was enlightening.

"Did you guys fight about Rod?"

"Oh yeah. He was disruptive to the whole family."

"Tell me about it."

"But especially to us, his parents. We couldn't help feeling that we'd failed him somehow. I mean, you raise three kids in the same house with the same parents. Same rules and expectations. It works for two, and completely fails for the third. Is that the parents' fault?"

"No."

"Well, I don't know."

"You put up with a lot of pain that Rod caused. It affected the entire family. You were more than tolerant until finally, you put an end to it. You did the right thing."

"Parenting isn't easy."

"But you set expectations for all of us. Rod didn't live up to them, and as hard as you guys tried, he failed and kept failing. So you made a difficult decision. It took guts, but you cut him from the family. Granted, it was tough on him and all of us. But in the long run it was in the family's best interest." He looked over at his dad. "I have to say, I admire that decision."

Their walking pace was causing his dad's breathing to become labored, so they slowed down.

"Rod's decisions in life were putting us all in danger," his dad said.

"Yep."

"So I did what I thought would keep the rest of you safe."

"Yep."

"But I couldn't give up on him. He is my son, just like you are."

Tom frowned. "What do you mean?"

"Your mother prayed and prayed for Rod. She kept asking for a miracle. For God to touch his heart and change his ways. For healing in our relationship. Despite what the courts said, she wanted him to still be part of our family."

Tom was silent. He had no idea. Of course, he was the oldest so by the time his parents were living through this phase with Rod, Tom had moved out on his own. They trudged a dozen more footsteps through the sand before his father went on. "Family is family, even if you don't agree with what they're doing. You do what you can to support and convince, and then you just let the Lord have His way. His way is the perfect way, you know."

"So, what happened?"

"Time passed and put all things in perspective. Rod's a grown man now. Is he perfect? No. Is he living the life I'd have chosen for him? No. But in the scheme of things, I had to decide if I'd rather be right and justified and tough, *or* if I wanted to be his dad. I couldn't do both. And after listening to your mother for years on end about forgiveness and the importance of family, it finally hit me. Family is more important."

"Let me get this straight. Are you saying, you and Rod are back in touch? You talk?"

"Yes."

"This is news to me."

"Mom and I talked about it and we didn't want to make you and Lori follow our lead. We figured, you're both adults and can come to the decision that's right for you. But we didn't want to influence you."

"Do you regret the decision you made? To cut ties, legally?"

"Sure I do. But I was all puffed up, thinking I was doing it for the right reasons. I was protecting my remaining children. One bad apple can spoil the whole batch. But as right as I was, as justified as I was — it's not what God teaches us. And it caused a terrible rift with the one woman God wanted me to love the most."

Tom shook his head, trying to clear it. This was news. But he also felt its importance, as if God himself was using his dad's visit to have this very conversation and get through to him. He'd been praying for guidance. What if this was the guidance he'd been asking for?

His dad continued, "I relied on the Bible during this time of transformation with your brother. There's a section in second Corinthians that I memorized: 'If anyone has caused you grief, you ought to forgive and comfort him. I urge you to reaffirm your love for him.' Yes, sir. Once I found that passage, I had my answer. It had been weighing heavy on my heart for years, and it was like God had directed it specifically at me."

Tom stopped walking, let his dad pass him a few steps, and faced the ocean. The relevance of this conversation was making his head spin. He'd respected his father his entire life. The way his father had handled Rod was family legend. Tom had always admired him for standing up and protecting his family, even though it was hard. Even though it was unpopular. It was tough but he made the right decision anyway.

Did his dad's approach for handling Rod influence the way Tom made up his mind to handle Jeremy? Absolutely, it did. Tom always knew that if he ever had to make a tough decision about the safety and well-being of his own family, he need only look to his own father for his role model. Just as Rod's cronies had brought direct danger to Tom's mother, someone in Jeremy's circle had brought direct danger to Stella. Just as the brick through the window was the tip of the iceberg of the damage and disaster Rod was capable of showering onto the family, so it was with Jeremy. He'd been incarcerated for ten years. Who knew what further danger and bad influence lurked close by?

Tom's family history had shown him the right way to handle Jeremy. His respect for his father made him secure in his knowledge that he was handling it correctly. Like father, like son. Despite the intense resistance from Marianne. All this time, he was sure she would eventually see reason.

Except ... Tom's father had changed his mind. He ultimately chose the more loving, forgiving approach endorsed by his mother. He forgave his errant son, invited him back into his life, his family.

This changed everything.

His father regretted his actions toward Rod. And if continued down the path he was going, Tom would undoubtedly regret his actions toward Jeremy. Especially if his stubborn determination to alienate his brother-in-law caused pain and anger in the one woman on this earth he loved more than life itself.

If he had destroyed his marriage because of his inability to consider that Marianne's way of handling it was the more Christian way — the more loving way, he'd never be able to forgive himself. *Family is family, even if you don't agree with what they're doing.*

An overwhelming feeling of understanding encompassed him. He looked up to the sky and whispered, "Thank You."

* * *

Tom found a few free moments between finishing his walk with his dad and getting Stella fed and dressed for tonight's performance. He got in the car and drove slowly to Jeremy's furniture store. The short drive over, he ran through his mind what he wanted to say. But when he arrived and parked the car and turned the engine off, he still had no idea.

He supposed he took after his dad more than he thought.

He sat quietly in the still car, and looked into the store through the plate-glass window. Jeremy was inside ringing up a customer.

Forgive. Comfort. Reaffirm.

That was God's message to him. He was here, ready to do it. But how? Easier said than done.

Jeremy's customer left and Jeremy moved to the back of the store. Tom sat another minute, than let out a deep breath. He prayed a quick, *Guide my words* and pushed himself out.

When he stepped through the door, Jeremy's head popped up. His expression, first welcoming, turned guarded. Understandable. Tom hadn't ever given him much reason to feel anything but guarded around him.

Tom walked with determination directly up to Jeremy, stopping in front of him. After a slight pause, he held out a hand. Jeremy looked down at it and recognized it for what it was. An offering. Jeremy took Tom's hand and they shook.

"Jeremy, I never thanked you properly for finding Stella."

Jeremy's eyebrows dove, creasing lines between his nose. "You don't have to thank me, ..."

Tom forged on. "Stella's lucky to have such a devoted uncle. And now I hear she's going to have an aunt too."

Jeremy's eyes widened slightly and he nodded.

"Kids can never have enough love in their lives. I wish you and Emma the best."

Jeremy shut his mouth and recovered. "I hope you all can come to the wedding. Nothing formal, really. This Wednesday evening at the Steeple Church, then back to my dad and Leslie's for a small reception."

"We'd be honored."

Jeremy stared. An awkward moment slipped by and Tom decided to take the "comfort" part of God's order to a new level. He leaned his body in, lifted his right arm and wrapped it around Jeremy's shoulders, pounding on his back. It couldn't really qualify as a hug, but maybe a bro-embrace. Hopefully it provided some small ounce of comfort to his brother-in-law.

"I haven't treated you right since you came home. I apologize for that and I hope that someday you can forgive me." He rushed on, despite Jeremy's attempt to object. "What I told you before? Forget it. You're welcome in our house. In our family."

He pulled away and headed for the door, murmuring, "See ya." He'd almost reached his destination when Jeremy said, "Tom?" Instead of a question he held his palms up and shrugged.

Tom smiled. "Read Second Corinthians."

Chapter Seventeen

On Wednesday morning, Tom was working on payroll behind the guest desk. Emma Slotky walked into the great room, holding a garment bag. She spotted him and came to a stop, staring intently. Tom came out from around the desk and held a hand out. "Can I help you with that?"

"No, that's all right. It's light." She held it a moment longer, then stepped over to the couch and laid it there. "Jeremy told me about your visit. I have to say we were both a little floored."

Tom nodded. "I had a heart-to-heart with a very wise man who helped me see the error of my ways."

Emma blinked. "It's not Jeremy you should have ever been mad at. It's my father. Or me, by connection."

"I'm not mad at you. Family is more important than being right. Or thinking you're right. Or having good reason to be a jerk." Tom clenched his mouth shut. It wasn't coming out right. It had been so eloquent when his dad had said it, and so clear in his mind. This was why he needed God to guide him. He reached out and put a hand on Emma's arm. "Regardless. I want to support and love you and Jeremy in your marriage, and I want us to be family. Can you forgive me for making things so difficult the last few months?"

Emma's face transformed into a happy sigh of relief. "Of course, Tom! I'm so glad to hear that. In fact," she turned and picked up the garment bag, "I'm going to leave this here. I got this for Stella to wear as flower girl, but I'll leave it to you and Marianne to decide if you want her to do it. Either way, we're just thrilled that you're coming to the wedding."

Tom gazed at it for a split second and the corner of his lips curled into a smile. "Do me a favor. Let's keep this as a surprise from Marianne for now, okay?"

She handed him the garment bag, stood on her tiptoes and gave him a very quick kiss on the cheek. With a "bye" she breezed out.

* * *

Wednesday evening, Marianne stood in the door of her tiny bedroom closet, staring at its contents. A wave of sadness rolled over her but she was determined to ignore it. This day should be one of the happiest of her life. Her dear Jeremy had found happiness and turned his life completely around. But instead, it was one of the saddest.

Shoving hanger after hanger aside, she huffed a deep breath. Tom should be taking her to this wedding, sharing in her happiness for her brother. Stella should be dressed in an adorable gown, holding her little basket of rose petals. Marianne should be coaching her on how to most daintily and delicately walk down the aisle, preparing it for the bride's arrival. Instead, she stood alone, ten pounds overweight, on the verge of tears, knowing that not a single garment in her closet would work. She'd either wear something comfortable that wasn't dressy enough, or she'd squeeze into something dressy and would barely be able to breathe, only to go to the ceremony alone.

She sighed and rubbed her eyes, determined to hold off the tears she felt just under the surface. Well, fair or not, she wasn't going to miss Jeremy's wedding. She simply wouldn't. She'd have to deal with Tom and his irrational anger later.

A dress would be most appropriate. Jeremy had said informal, but he was wearing a tux, and Emma was wearing a white wedding gown, so the guests should be dressed in kind. The only problem was, she hadn't worn a dress, other than a summer sundress in several years, and it was too chilly still, in April, for a sundress. Not to mention, her sundresses were ancient, probably out of style, and possibly raggedy.

She dug further back and pulled out one or two slightly more formal dresses. A quick check of the tags proved her fear — she was up a size or in some cases, two, too big to wear them comfortably. She threw one of her skinny dresses down on the closet floor and groaned. She should've made the time to go clothes shopping today. What had been so important today that she couldn't slip away for an hour to make sure she was adequately dressed for her brother's most important night of his life?

A rustling behind her had her whirling around in a panic. Tom stood, clad in dress pants and button-down shirt, and was looking in the mirror, struggling with a tie. "Give me a hand?" he said distractedly. "I can't remember the last time I've had to tie one of these things."

She stared, wide-eyed, then walked up behind him, shooing his hands away from the tie and taking it over herself. When they were first married and Tom had a corporate job in an office, she'd tied his ties for him every morning. There was something intimate about putting the final touches on her businessman. Since they'd bought the Inn, his suit-wearing days were about as over as her dress-wearing days. However, she noticed with a humph, his suit appeared to fit as perfectly as the day he bought it.

She finished the job and he turned around and before she could even think, he laid his lips on hers and ran his hands up and down her arms, slowly, cherishing her lips with their warmth. He pulled away and she was breathless. She turned away to get a hold of herself. She turned back. "You look nice. What's the occasion?"

Surprise flickered across his face. "Jeremy and Emma's wedding."

"You're going?" She didn't mean her tone to come out accusatorially, but there it was. And he'd noticed it too, based on the brief damage on his expression.

"Yes."

Miracles never ceased. Well, as much as she appreciated him going, he'd better not ruin it. She expected him to be supportive and keep his negative opinions to himself.

She turned back to her closet. "Unfortunately, I don't have anything to wear."

He came up behind her and peered in. He reached in and pulled out a turquoise cotton sundress, the bodice and straps highlighted by a white lace applique.

She shook her head. "It's sleeveless. Too chilly."

He stuck his bottom lip out and looked into her closet again. With half a second's examination, he pulled out a denim cropped Western jacket with three-quarter length sleeves, front welt pockets and princess seams. She frowned at it. "Denim? This is a wedding. Too casual."

"Try it on together. You'll look beautiful."

She sighed, then figured it was a better combination than she had come up with. She quickly undressed, slipped the dress on, and the jacket on top. She left the jacket unbuttoned and something about the lace applique gave it a little dressiness. The denim would keep her warm from the chill, it was a dress and it fit. Home run.

She looked at him shyly. "Thanks, Tom."

He smiled, grabbed his suit jacket and left the room. She heard him a few minutes later in Stella's room. Stella was excited about something, judging from her giggles. She paused outside her daughter's door, listening to the laughter and excitement, mingled with Tom's deeper voice. She tapped on the door and opened it.

Tom was kneeling behind Stella, zipping up her dress. Stella was bouncing on her tiptoes, anxious for him to finish. She twirled around and barely contained her words, "Look at my new dress, Mommy! It's for Uncle Jeremy and Aunt Emma's wedding. They're getting married! And we're all going to watch, and I have a new dress!"

Yes, it was new. Marianne had never laid eyes on it before. Not only was it new, it was beyond dressy. It was a deep island blue taffeta with a fitted bodice, sleeveless arms, and studded rhinestones along the neckline. The knee-length skirt was full and pleated, complete with a lovely fabric bow around the waist. Stella looked gorgeous.

She stared, mouth open, from her daughter to her husband. "What the heck is going on? Did your parents bring this dress for her? Why is this the first time I'm seeing it?" She walked in the room and took the beautiful skirt in between her fingers. "You look like a princess, baby."

Tom stood. "We better go or we'll be late to the wedding." Stella ran past her, followed closely by Tom. She grabbed his arm and said in a loud whisper, "What?"

He smiled. "I never should've said that Stella couldn't go to the wedding. I'm sorry."

This complete 180 by Tom confused her. But gave her a cautious sense of optimism. She shook her head as she followed her family out to the car.

* * *

They drove a few miles off the island to a white frame church, boasting a tall white steeple that soared into the clouds, nestled in a small valley filled with trees. It was like a fairytale church. They walked inside and Marianne immediately picked up on the whispered excitement of the wedding. She saw her dad, dressed in a tux, Leslie proudly holding his arm. She waved and they made their way over.

"Well, don't you look handsome, Daddy?" Marianne said with a smile and gave him a kiss, then wiped her lipstick off his cheek. She leaned in and gave an air kiss to Leslie who looked beautiful and cool as ever in a peach satin dress.

"I'm not only the father of the groom but I'm the best man," Hank said, and he couldn't hide the grin from his lips. Marianne inhaled softly, put her hand to her mouth, then had to fight back a tear. She gazed over at Leslie and they exchanged a knowing nod. This was only true because of Leslie. It was because of his dad's bride that Hank had forgiven Jeremy last summer for the terrible troubles he'd caused the family. The fact that Jeremy had found love, and Hank was serving as best man was a testament to the love and forgiveness that only God can accomplish.

As she shared a few words with her dad, she noticed Tom leaning over and whispering something to Stella. He rose and said, "We'd better get our seats, huh?"

Her dad held a crooked arm out to Marianne and she took it and allowed him to lead her, followed by her small family, to the second row on the groom's side. She looked up at the altar, covered with colorful spring flowers in teals, pinks and greens. The pipe organ saturated the room with heavy blasts of classic music.

They sat, and after a moment, Leslie scooted in beside them, followed by her daughter, Jasmine. Marianne came to her feet, fussed over her younger stepsister and thanked her for coming. Jasmine looked adorable in a form-fitting pink dress. She was a senior at a college in New York. How very sweet of her to get away in the middle of a week, when she was surely approaching final exams, to support her stepbrother. After she sat, Marianne leaned over and told her so.

"Hey, I feel somewhat responsible for them getting this far. I wouldn't want to miss the wedding!"

"What do you mean?"

Jasmine beamed. "When I finished last semester, I came and stayed with Mom and Hank for a couple weeks. Jeremy and Emma were dating but Jeremy was thinking about breaking up with her, you know the *noble* thing because her father didn't like him. He thought he was making her life easier by backing out of it."

"Really."

"Yep. I set him straight. And now look — they're getting married!"

"Good for you, Jasmine."

"Maybe I'll start working on them to name their first baby after me." They chuckled together and then Stella announced, "Mommy, I have to go to the restroom."

She nodded and started to get up, but Tom put his hand on her arm. "I'll go with her. I saw the door in the back."

She frowned. Tom taking Stella to the ladies' room? She couldn't remember a time he'd ever done that, if Marianne were available. Hmm. Maybe he was having a change of heart. He had come to the wedding, allowed Stella to come, and even apologized about it. She'd have to talk to him later and find out just how far this turnaround went.

The organ music changed then. Marianne recognized the opening of the traditional "Here Comes the Bride" song. She turned in her seat, hoping to find Stella. No way would she want to miss the processional of the bridesmaids and the bride. Just then, Tom slid back into the pew beside her.

"Oh good, I didn't want Stella to miss …," Coming to a halt, she blinked at him. "Where's Stella?" Her daughter hadn't reappeared when her husband did.

Tom smiled and pointed — to the back of the sanctuary. Marianne gave him a confused glare, and then turned in her seat to face the back. Along with the sound of "ahhhhs" from the crowd, she saw it.

Stella, in her island blue sequined dress, held a basket of rose petals and walked down the aisle, tossing them randomly, smiling gleefully. When she was still a few rows away, a young woman wearing the same color, in a similar style dress, held a bouquet and followed Stella, walking determinedly in slow, methodical steps. Emma's maid of honor.

"Stella's the flower girl!" Jasmine said happily. "She looks adorable."

Marianne tried to pull her mouth shut from her surprise and tore her gaze away from Stella long enough to look at Tom. He knew. He wasn't surprised at all. In fact, he was so much more on top of this than she was. That dress, which matched perfectly with the bridal party, hadn't come from his parents. Tom must have okayed Stella taking part in Jeremy's wedding, and kept it as a surprise from her. But why?

Stella approached their row and turned in, so excited and happy she was fairly bouncing as she walked. Marianne leaned down and wrapped her in a hug. "You did great, honey! Perfect job." Stella nodded, exuding happiness in the most magical gown she'd ever worn.

Then, Jeremy and her dad stepped through a doorway and took a few steps to the altar, where they stood facing the audience. Marianne's heart flooded with happiness for him, so glad that he was experiencing this moment after all he'd been through.

Emma's bridesmaid made it to her destination, turned and faced the congregation as well. Then everyone stood. It was Emma's turn.

She made her way down the aisle, not on her dad's arm, but on her mom's, who was dressed one shade lighter than Stella. Emma's dress was a simple but exquisite halter-necked chiffon wedding gown. The A-Line hem fell just to her knee, and her neck was draped with beads and sparkles. Her mountain of brown curls was worn up in a loose, wispy bun and the dress flowed gracefully with each step she took. A short lace veil covered her face.

Marianne dragged her eyes away from her beauty for a second to focus on the groom. Jeremy stood transfixed, motionless and stunned.

Emma approached him and the music settled down. The minister asked, "Who gives this young woman to this man in holy matrimony?"

Emma's mother reached up, removed the veil from Emma's face and leaned in to kiss her cheek. She turned to the minister and said, "I do."

When they all settled into their seats, Tom tapped her arm. Marianne looked over. He whispered in her ear. "Can I steal you away for five minutes or less?"

"*Now?*" She almost refused. She didn't want to miss Jeremy's ceremony. But the look on Tom's face was so intense and focused that she knew it was important. And considering the surprises he'd already bestowed upon her this evening, she had to admit she was curious to find what was next. She nodded and they stood and started squeezing out of the aisle. When she crossed in front of Leslie, she made eye contact and pointed at Stella. Leslie nodded, an understanding between two mothers.

Tom led her out the back, and into a small room where he closed the door. He turned to her and gently took both her hands in his. Then he brushed away a lock of hair that had fallen into her eyes, took a deep breath and let it out. "I love you, Marianne."

She almost responded the same automatically, but she held back. He'd dragged her out of her brother's wedding to tell her something, and she felt quite certain there was more.

"I've always loved you, and I've always admired you. You're fiercely loyal to those you love, and you're the best wife and mother I know."

She bit her lip. "Thank you, T…" but he squeezed her hands, stopping her.

"Let me get this out. You listen and I'll talk. I owe you that."

She blinked quickly, her emotion about to take form in her eyes. She nodded.

"The last few months have been difficult. We got through a terrible trauma but we let it tear our relationship apart. We didn't bond together in adversity, like we should have. I take full responsibility for that. You know why I took such a strong stance on keeping Stella away from Jeremy. You know I thought I was doing it with the best intentions. But I was wrong, and you were right. I should've listened to you and followed your example from the very beginning. I was stubborn in my decision. I disregarded your feelings like they weren't valid. That's how justified I thought I was. I didn't want to admit that sometimes opening up your heart and accepting and forgiving lead to the right path."

Marianne couldn't believe what she was hearing. This man she loved had caused her so much pain. But she'd prayed over and over for a resolution for their marriage and here it was. She squeezed her eyes shut and said a silent *thank you* to God.

"I'm sorry, Marianne. I want to be more like you. Jeremy deserves our love and support. He's Stella's uncle. He's family. I always knew that, but I needed a reminder. Can you forgive me for how I handled this? Can you love me like you did before? Can you give me another chance?"

"Yes. Yes, of course. I love you, Tom."

He let go of her hands and wrapped her in a tight embrace. His shoulders shook and she breathed in his scent and his warmth. When they separated, he wiped his eyes. She'd never known him to cry before. She was always the one with tears in her eyes. He laughed and shook his head. "I'm sorry."

She pulled him back close. "I'm sorry, too."

"For?"

"For separating myself from you. I didn't know how to deal with the distance that kept forming between us. I was so angry at you. I let a huge separation come between us and I filled it with work. I worked really hard on that play, but in some ways, it was an escape from you. From our problems that were driving me crazy. I couldn't control that, so I buried myself into producing something new. Next time — if there *is* a next time — we'll work together better. We won't ever let a disagreement drive such a huge wedge between us again." She looked into his eyes, and they were clear of moisture, but overloaded with joy.

"I know we have some work to do to get back to where we were before," Tom said. "If you want, we can get some help from our pastor."

Marianne's heart felt like it would explode. "Really? You'd do that?"

"For us, yes. To heal us so we can move forward, stronger than ever. I love you, Marianne, and I never want to lose you."

Marianne gazed at him, her Tom, the one she'd loved for so long, so grateful that he was back. "Have you ever read in the Bible about God's perfect plan for married couples? The role of the husband and the role of the wife?"

"Maybe …"

"I'll share that with you later." She pulled him towards her and laid her lips on his. Although they'd kissed probably a thousand times in their life together, it hadn't been recently. And this time, she was glad to notice, her heart raced and her pulse danced, reacting to their closeness. "I love you, Tom. It's over. We're both committing to getting us back, and we'll get there."

They took a minute to hold each other, then headed back to the wedding. They held hands as they tiptoed back to their seats on the pew. As she passed, Leslie patted Marianne on the shoulder and winked with a broad smile.

They'd missed most of the minister's message, but she'd watch it later on video. It was soon time for a small surprise that Marianne had thrown together for her brother and his bride. As Jeremy and Emma moved to the side to light the Unity Candle, Roxanne and Tieg stepped up to the center of the altar and sang their beautiful love song duet from the musical, "Till There Was You." The bride and groom sought Marianne out in the congregation and smiled their thanks.

Eventually, the minister announced, "You may kiss your bride." Not only did Jeremy reach for Emma, but Tom reached for Marianne, wrapped his arms around her and laid a kiss on her so deep and heartfelt that she felt dizzy. He dipped her backward like a ballroom dancer and even though she heard snickers and giggles in the pew around them, she didn't protest.

After all, she deserved her happy ending as well.

THE END

Excerpt: Book 4, Pawleys Island Paradise
(currently untitled)

Chapter One

Jasmine Malone was dashing out the door of her dorm room when her cell phone buzzed with a text notification. She groaned. She was already late for her appointment with Susan, and really didn't have the time to stop and see who was texting her. Besides, last time she'd had her massage appointment, Susan warned her that if she was late again, she'd still end the appointment on time, so she wouldn't be running five or ten minutes late with every appointment the rest of the day.

Jasmine flew out of the dorm, raced to her car and jumped in. Pointedly ignoring whoever was trying to contact her, she shoved into drive and was on her way, only slightly above the speed limit.

Susan was a lifesaver. Jasmine had discovered her two years ago at the salon, and had reserved monthly massages with her exclusively ever since. Her life as a busy college student majoring in Fashion Design and Marketing at Cornell University landed her stress directly in her neck and shoulders, and an hour with Susan once a month kept her loose and relaxed. Now, with finals done, all that was keeping her from graduation was the arrival of her parents.

Both of them. That is, her mom and new husband Hank, and her dad. Solo. Since his relationship with his girlfriend which had broken up their marriage, was now splitsville.

She had no idea how to deal with this dysfunctional family dynamic. Hence, one last appointment with Susan.

She screeched into the salon parking lot and ran up a flight of stairs to the salon. Was she late? She glanced at her phone and saw that no, she was right on time. The receptionist asked for her name.

"Jasmine Malone. I have an appointment with Susan."

The girl tapped on her keyboard and looked up. "Oh, didn't you get our text? Susan isn't here today. "

Jasmine frowned, hit the messaging icon on her phone and saw that indeed, the salon had sent her something. She opened the message quickly. "Your appointment this afternoon will be with Dax instead of Susan."

"Wait, w——, Dax? What exactly is a Dax?" She pulled her attention from her phone to the woman behind the desk.

"Dax is one of our licensed masseuses. He's very good, actually."

Jasmine glared at her and the girl's cheeks turned a shade of pink. "What happened to Susan?"

"She had a family emergency." The receptionist cleared her throat, patted her cheeks and let her eyes rest on Jasmine. "Would you like your massage with Dax?"

Jasmine sighed. On the one hand, she had a rule about her masseuses: females only. She wasn't entirely sure why. But she thought it had something to do with the fact that under the flimsy sheet, she'd be totally naked. And the masseuse would, of course, have his hands all over her.

And she just wasn't comfortable with that.

On the other hand, she was tense and tight thinking about entertaining her parents, this first time she'd seen them together since their divorce last summer. And it was her, who'd brought them together. Well, her graduation.

So, she did a mental coin toss and decided, "Okay, yes. Dax it is."

"He'll be out in just a second."

Jasmine nodded and sat down, picked up a fashion mag and started flipping through it. A few minutes passed and she heard a deep, rumbling voice that caused a trembling deep in her stomach. "Jasmine?"

She looked up and her heart jumped in her throat. Tall, lean, thin-hipped. Curly brown hair, shoulder length. Smoldering brown eyes and just a hint of whisker on his chin and lip. He was dressed in white scrubs and his dark skin glistened in contrast.

The man was gorgeous. Her voice had disappeared. As had her mind. What had he said?

"Jasmine?" he said again, this time looking directly at her.

Jasmine darted her head around the waiting room. There was only one other person sitting, besides her, and it was a woman her mom's age. She cleared her throat and said a quick prayer for God to help her act normal and not embarrass herself. She had, after all, seen her fair share of handsome men before. She'd done a fashion internship in Paris last summer, for goodness sake. She'd dressed male models and helped them change clothes backstage at fashion shows. She could do this.

Of course, 90% of those men were gay. But still.

"Yes," she said, probably a trifle too loud. She cleared her throat again and said softer, "That's me." She rose and approached him.

He smiled and held his hand out. "Good afternoon. I'm Dax."

Heat flooded her cheeks and she knew she was blushing. "Nice to meet you," she muttered.

"Right this way."

She followed him. They went through a labyrinth of narrow hallways until Dax opened a door and led her into a small room with the massage table in the middle, a chair in the corner and a counter and sink in one corner. "Have a seat, please," he said, motioning to the chair. He pulled out a folder and glanced at it. "One hour relaxation massage."

"Yes."

"You get them monthly? Very good, very good."

Her heart rate increased. "Can we just get started?"

His head darted up. "Of course. Do you have any problem areas I should be aware of?"

She took a deep breath. "Not really. I just finished finals so I'm sure my neck and shoulders are tight. All that studying, you know."

He nodded. "Oh, you're a student?"

"Not for long. I'm graduating tomorrow from Cornell."

He smiled and the sheer beauty of it almost made her swoon. "Congratulations."

"Thanks," she said and looked down at her lap.

"I'd love to go to college, but haven't had the chance yet."

She looked back up at him. "Didn't you go to massage school?"

He nodded. "Yes, that was an eleven-month program. Very intense. But I'd like to start my own massage studio someday. Hire several therapists and offer all kinds of massage. I'd need a Business degree to do that."

Okay, this was helping. Her heart rate was slowing and she felt a little more relaxed, getting to know him a little.

"I'll leave and you take everything off. Lay on the table face down and drape the sheet over you."

So much for feeling relaxed. Her pulse flew through her veins and she saw a few spots in front of her eyes. "You know, I'm not sure I can do this."

He gave her a concerned look. "What do you mean?"

She gave a nervous chuckle. "I mean, you're a man." She exhaled air. "Well, obviously you're a man. You know that, and I know that. But I've only ever had massages from women. So I'm not sure I'm comfortable with …"

"Ahhh. You're modest. That's okay. I won't see anything private, I promise. And there are benefits from getting massages from a man." He held up all ten fingers for her to see. "Strong hands. They can go forever."

Oh boy. Just the thought of Dax's strong hands and long fingers all over her body, going forever, caused her face to flood heat again. "I just remembered. I'm late for an appointment. I'm sorry."

She stood and headed for the door. But his face fell and he looked actually … heartbroken. Crestfallen. She stopped.

"No, no, it's okay. I understand." His head dipped as he made a notation in her file and closed it. "Thank you for your time." He turned and started toward the door.

Something in his dejected stance gave her a change of heart. "Dax, it's not you. Really."

He held a hand up and shook his head. "It's tough for male masseuses. Men don't often want to be massaged by a man. They prefer a woman. And women often don't want to be massaged by a man either. Until I build up a clientele I don't get a lot of business. But without doing a lot of business, I can't build up my clientele." He shrugged and opened the door.

"I'll do it," she said quickly before she changed her mind. "I'll do the massage."

"You will?" His beaming smile looked so happy she almost closed her eyes to block the view. A smoldering Dax was hard enough to resist. But a happy, ecstatic Dax was nearly impossible.

"Yes. I'll get undressed and scoot under the sheet. Give me ten minutes. But no touching anywhere that you shouldn't, you got that?"

"Of course not! I'm a professional." He gave an excited little bow and backed out the door.

Made in the USA
Columbia, SC
20 March 2018